PUMPKIN SPICE SACRIFICE

MURDER IN THE MIX 3

∅

ADDISON MOORE

HOLLIS THATCHER PRESS, LTD.

MURDER IN THE MIX

ADDISON MOORE

Pumpkin Spice Sacrifice

BOOK DESCRIPTION

My name is Lottie Lemon and I see dead people. Okay, so I rarely see dead people, mostly I see furry creatures of the dearly departed variety—but today seems to be that rare exception. Worse yet, that good-looking ghost just so happens to look just like my friend, Everett, and it refuses to leave his side. I'm petrified of losing Everett, so much so that I too refuse to leave his side, which of course doesn't exactly bode well with my newly minted boyfriend, Noah Fox, who is just as comely as his surname suggests. After two horrific murders just took place in our small town of Honey Hollow, I'm ready to put the last few months behind me, but when I come across another gruesome discovery, my entire world comes crashing down on me once again.

Lottie Lemon has a brand new bakery to tend to, a budding romance with perhaps one too many suitors, and she has the supernatural ability to see the dead—which are always harbingers for ominous things to come. Throw in the occasional ghost of the human variety, a string of murders, and her insatiable thirst for justice, and you'll have more chaos than you know what to do with.

Living in the small town of Honey Hollow can be murder.

CHAPTER 1

I see dead people.

Okay, so more often than not, I see furry creatures of the dearly departed variety, and, believe you me, they are not a good omen for their previous owner —which is where I usually spot the fuzzy little phantasms. They seem to appear just before something horrific is about to befall the aforementioned previous owner, and up until just a few months ago, that never involved a fatality. However, after Merilee Simonson, my old landlord, and Hunter Fisher, my old good friend, both met with an untimely demise, I'm beginning to see a homicidal trend brewing here. And trust me, I'm the last person on the planet who wants to see a homicidal trend percolating in the cauldron of life—especially after I was the number one suspect in Merilee's death. Not that there are many dead bodies lying around in our tiny corner of Vermont. Honey Hollow is known more for its fall splendor, which we're smack-dab in the middle of. And it's as homey and cozy as its name suggests.

But, at the moment, I'm not looking at a long-deceased precious creature. I'm looking at a warm-blooded, very much alive and full of mischief, Himalayan, who happens to belong to yours truly. Pancake was gifted to me over a year ago by my best friend's grandmother, Nell. She had a hard time deciding between two cute kitties and brought them both home, citing she would keep the one I didn't choose. Of course, I couldn't resist. I took one look at those big silver-blue eyes and fell instantly and madly in love. I named my sweet angel—a far too generous moniker, considering I'm staring down at a pile of down feathers floating in a five-foot vicinity—*Pancake* and Nell named hers Waffles.

"Pancake Lemon, I am going to gift you a middle

name, so I can scold you properly. If you keep this up, I'll be forced to give you two—or three."

He glances up at me, bored from the sofa. That butter yellow fur looks almost silver with the sunlight streaking across his back. His nose and the tip of his tail have a bit of a coffee-colored stain to them that just adds to how handsome he really is.

"Oh, stop it, Lottie." Lainey breezes in with an oversized box in her arms marked *bedroom*. Lainey is my older sister, and even though the Lemons adopted me when I was just days old, Lainey and I still manage to share the same caramel waves and light hazel eyes. "Pancake wasn't responsible for the feathered carnage. I may have done that. The darn pillow snagged on a loose nail on the railing. Everett is fixing the culprit right now."

No sooner does she breeze right past me than the sound of a hammer dealing out a couple of hearty blows echoes through my new rental. Pancake looks to the door with pure boredom before closing his eyes for his evening nap.

"Sorry, buddy." I give his head a quick scratch. "I should have known you weren't capable. It would take far too much energy to make the place look like you got into a fight with a canary—and won."

Keelie grunts her way inside, hoisting in the last of the dining room chairs, her blonde curls bouncing with every charged step. Keelie Turner is as perky and adorable as her name suggests.

"I see how it goes." She scoffs my way. "We do all the work while you snuggle up with the cat." She blows Pancake a kiss. "How about we trade places, Lot? I'm zonked." Keelie and I have been fast friends ever since pre-school. Nell is her grandmother, and so she's always felt like a bit of an aunt to both Pancake and Waffles.

Nell Sawyer owns half of Honey Hollow. She owns the Honey Pot Diner, where Keelie works. And she happens to own the Cutie Pie Bakery and Cakery, where I'm more than happily employed. It's been my dream for as far back as I can remember to have a bakery of my own, and the fact Nell has given me complete charge of the place makes me feel pretty darn lucky.

Noah strides in and gifts me a crooked grin, his biceps bulging to mouthwatering degrees as he sets a box marked *just stuff* down onto the dining room table. Noah Corbin Fox is a private investigator that recently moved to Honey Hollow, and I happened to run into him at his office. I may have thought he was a loan officer and tried my best to wrangle some finances from him for the bakery. As it turns out, Noah ended up gifting the bakery the appliances it needed with the money left from his father's estate. Apparently, his father was a swindler, and Noah wanted nothing to do with the money.

He strides my way and wraps his strong arms around my waist. His lids hood low on cue. "Hey, beautiful." Noah dots my lips with a kiss, and every last part of me melts like chocolate sitting over a double boiler hungry with heat. Noah has expressive green eyes and a naughty crooked grin that makes any and every female in a five-mile radius do a lust-filled double take. He also has a face that looks as if the Almighty himself spent a millennium chiseling it to perfection, and when he smiles at me, I feel as if we're the only two people in the world. Of course, he has both brain and brawn going for him, hot and heavy. There is no contesting the fact that Noah Fox is all man. He's brilliant, and reliable, and will most definitely make the perfect husband one day.

My lips twitch with a smile of their own. Noah and I have only just begun our journey together, considering we met in September and it's just now *November*, but I'd say yes in an impulsive second if he popped the question. He's insanely gorgeous and sincere to a fault. And his best trait by far is that he's extremely protective of my safety. I may or may not have gotten involved with an open homicide investigation that he was working on a few weeks back and almost got myself killed in the process, but that's all in the past.

"I can't thank you enough for helping." I brush a careful kiss over his lips and linger. I'd much rather be doing exactly this than hauling a mountain of boxes into my new living room.

Someone clears their throat from the door, and we look over to find Essex Everett Baxter, the honorable judge who happened to side in my favor when my landlords hauled me to small claims court back in September. Everett was just filling in that day. He usually sees much meatier cases, which involve full-blown juries and require harsh sentencings that lead to lengthy prison stays. It sounds terribly exciting—as long as I'm on the right side of the law—and one day I fully intend to pick his brain about it. Everett and Noah used to be stepbrothers back in high school when Everett's mother was married to Noah's swindler of a father. And as fate would have it, some of the money that was given to me for the bakery just so happened to be swindled from her. I didn't know it at the time, and Everett apparently gave his green light to the endeavor.

Everett is younger than you might expect for a judge. He's thirty-two, and Noah is thirty-one to my twenty-six. We all went to dinner at the Honey Pot last night after we did an initial haul of boxes and clothing. Turns out, Everett's closet is just as full as mine. But that doesn't say a lot, considering the fact the wardrobe of a baker is pretty basic. After dinner, we talked at length about our lives. I told Everett about my adoption—Noah already knew that part, but I kept mum on the New

York debacle that occurred during and post my college years at Columbia.

Last month, when Noah mentioned that a couple of homes were for rent on his street, Everett came with us to check them out. He liked the one next door so much he *bought* it. Noah lives across the street, adjacent to my cute little white clapboard house with its white picket fence porch and cheery red door. It's so homey, I feel like I've lived here for years, and already I don't ever want to move.

"That's it." Everett lands the last box onto the dining room table. He nods over to Keelie and Lainey who both just plopped onto the sofa next to Pancake. "Thanks for everything, guys. You didn't have to help me move, too. Helping Lemon would have been more than enough." His lips pull back with a temporal grin. Everett doesn't smile much, has little to say, and seems to be made up of pure testosterone. His hair is dark, his eyes are a glacial blue, and he wears a suit just about every day of the week—with the exception of this one. Apparently, women have been falling all over him for eons, and now that I've had a chance to witness the debauchery first-hand, I can honestly say it's not a pretty sight. One day I fully expect to see a knock-down, drag-out brawl in his honor. Everett admitted that he's not the relationship type, and he has an entire string of exes to prove it. "I'll see you guys soon."

"Oh no, you don't!" I pull both Everett and Noah along as I herd everyone into the kitchen. I wanted to sleep here last night, but Lainey wouldn't hear of me staying in an empty house with nothing more than an air mattress and my sweet cat. Lainey was nice enough to let me live with her for the last few months after the Simonson sisters gave me the boot. "We're going to make a toast," I say, pulling the champagne flutes from a box and setting them over the creamy marble island that's been vying for a coveted position in my heart ever since I laid eyes on it. And, believe me, this baby has gotten it.

Keelie opens the fridge and groans. "You're missing a key ingredient, Lottie. No champs."

"Sorry," I say, reaching for the fruit-flavored seltzer water and distributing it evenly into five glasses. "I'll make it up to you next time." I give a sly wink to Noah because I plan on making it up to him far sooner than that.

Lainey helps disperse the flutes, and soon we're lifting our arms.

"To new beginnings with wonderful neighbors." I raise my glass and tip my head toward Noah and Everett.

Pancake lets out a howl from the next room, and we all share a laugh on his behalf.

"To new beginnings," the four of them chime before imbibing.

Noah takes a breath, his chest expanding the size of a door, and I can't help but bite down on my lower lip. Noah and I haven't taken that next step in our relationship yet. Heck, I haven't even seen the inside of his rental home yet. We've been that busy. But once things settle down, I'm looking forward to rectifying just about everything with that tall, dark-haired, dimpled, headstrong detective.

Noah gives a wayward glance my way, and a heated line bisects my stomach on cue. Noah Fox is welcome to send a wayward glance my way as often as he likes. And now that we're within a stone's throw of one another, I expect one on the regular.

"I've got an announcement to make," Noah says as he looks to Everett and me.

Everett's chest thumps with a dry laugh. "Don't tell me I've chased you out of the neighborhood so soon."

"Not funny," I say, wrapping my arms around Noah. "You're not moving, are you?"

"Well"—his head inches back, and his dark brows dance over his eyes like caterpillars—"I sort of am, sort of not. Captain Turner called last night and offered me a position with the sheriff's department."

"*What?*" I shriek as the rest of the room breaks out into cheers. Noah worked as a detective back in Cincinnati but was fired after he discharged his weapon at the man his ex was cheating on him with. A completely understandable malfeasance in my opinion. I hop up and crash a congratulatory kiss over his lips. "Is it true?"

"Yes, it's true." He looks to Keelie. "Your dad is a great guy. He said I could work alongside Detective Fairbanks since the department is short on staff, and once the probation period is through, he'll evaluate and see if I can get in for good."

A pang of grief hits me, for no other reason than jealousy. Detective Fairbanks just so happens to be a gorgeous leggy redhead with the face and body of a supermodel.

"But what about your office next to the bank?" The feeble protest sounds both foolish and rife with spite just coming from my lips.

"I'm keeping it for now. That way if things don't work out, I'll have a fallback plan."

Everett raises his glass. "They'll work out." He frowns as if they wouldn't. "They didn't call you the golden kid in high school for nothing."

I'm about to demand all the dirty *deets* concerning my newly minted boyfriend's high school hazy days when Pancake hisses from the next room.

"He's been acting up ever since we set foot in this place," I say, glancing over. It's an open floor plan, but with the endless tower of boxes, we've effectively walled him in.

Lainey rolls her eyes. "And you've been blaming that poor cat for everything. How about I take Pancake home with me?" She gives a sly wink. "I think he likes me better, anyhow."

"You wish." Another hiss emits from the sofa as I detangle myself from Noah. "I'll be right back."

Keelie starts in, a mile a minute, about how she knew all about Noah's big surprise and the fact that she put in a good word for him. I'm sure Jack, *Captain Turner*—I've grown up with the man as a second father, so I can't seem to call him Captain—anyway, I'm positive he's seen for himself what a great investigator Noah is. I'm thrilled he thought of him to fill the need on the force. I'm not thrilled that he's working with Detective Redheaded Barbie.

Another hiss expires and I glance over to the sofa, but there's not a sign of Pancake.

I do a quick sweep of the vicinity and spot his rust tipped tail swishing back and forth from under the couch.

Odd. Pancake's tail never swishes. In fact, the last time it did so, he thought he was defending me against a giant predator—aka the tiniest, cutest little mouse with big brown eyes you've ever seen.

The door has been open all day. I bet an entire fleet of mice ran in. Just perfect. I happen to detest the thought of mice anywhere near where I sleep or eat, no matter how cute their big brown eyes might be.

Laughter erupts from the kitchen as Keelie continues to regale them with one bubbly story after the next.

"Come here, you." I get down on my knees and do my best to excavate Pancake, but judging by the way his claws are fighting every inch of it, he's not a willing party. "No, no, no, you have to love this house. I love it so much I want to live here forever, and if that pans out, I can't have you clawing your way through the furniture. This is your home, too, you know." I amble back to my feet with Pancake squirming to get out of my arms, but I'm too stubborn to let him go. He cranes his neck past me and hisses so hard I turn in a dizzying spin, fully expecting to find a human-sized rat, but it's not a rat by far. "*Everett*," I pant, closing my eyes for a second. "You scared the daylights out of me."

"I did?" a deep voice booms from behind, and I spin back on my heels to see the handsome judge on his way toward the door.

"How'd you do that?" I marvel for a moment.

"Do what?" he says as Lainey and Keelie come over and offer me a quick embrace before heading out into the icy autumn air.

"Congratulations again!" Keelie calls out as they make their way to their cars.

I frown over at Everett "You *know*..." I glance over

my shoulder and spot those glowing blue eyes of his staring right back at me and let out a sharp howl.

"Whoa." Noah comes over and takes Pancake from me. "I think your mom is in desperate need of a nap."

"And maybe vodka," I say under my breath. And that's a big deal, considering the fact I don't make a practice to drink. Standing behind me a good five feet is *Everett*. For a second, I scan the vicinity for a mirror because standing in front of me a good five feet is Everett as well. "You wouldn't happen to have a twin, would you?" I ask weakly.

Noah pulls me in, his brows pinched in a vexingly sexy V as his concern brews heavy. "Are you feeling all right?"

"I'm"—I look to Everett, the one standing by the door, as he pulls on his jacket—"I guess maybe I am tired." So tired I'm hallucinating! Good grief. Unless, of course…

I suck in a sharp breath and turn my head abruptly to meet up with those piercing blue eyes of Everett's questionable twin, and it's then I note the fact I can see my television right through his vellum-like body.

"Oh no," I whimper as Noah slips an arm around my waist and pulls me in.

"I think it's officially past your bedtime."

"Right." I look back and catch Everett, the solid,

earthbound version just as he's about to step out of the house.

"I guess I'll see you tomorrow night at the Endeavor awards ceremony." He grimaces at the two of us. "I promised Collette I'd go. She's really excited. I couldn't say no."

"You never say no," Noah is quick to remind him.

"Yes, for sure I'll see you th-there," I stammer.

"Good." Everett tweaks his brows. "Collette said to remind you that her boss likes pumpkin spice everything."

"Good thing for me, I'm bringing just about everything."

He gives a dark chuckle. "Sounds good, Lemon. Goodnight, neighbor." He gives a brief wave as he closes the door behind him. And just as I'm about to glance back at that specter bearing his resemblance, he strides right past Noah and me. He turns his head and looks at me with those same serious eyes, that all too familiar stern expression firmly on his face, and gives a slight wave as he walks right through the door and out into the night.

"Hey"—Noah pecks a kiss just under my ear—"I think I'm going to scoot so you can get some rest. You're starting to look pale. I think maybe you should turn in early."

"Oh, I will." Although I don't think I'll be able to

catch a wink. "Say, whatever happened to Everett's father?" I've heard Everett mention his mother and sister. I never thought to ask about his father.

"He died a while back. Everett was in junior high, I think. It was right before my own father came into the picture." He growls at the memory. "Why? Did he say something?"

"No, actually, I don't think he did."

Noah shrugs it off. "I wouldn't think so. His old man was off the table as far as topics went. At least back in the day. I think they had some sort of falling out just before he bit the big one."

"That's too bad."

"It is. Once someone's gone, that's it. You don't get a chance to make amends. You don't get to *see* them again —at least on this side." He leans in and lands a gentle kiss to my lips before backing away slowly. "I'll be in Ashford tomorrow filling out some last-minute paper-work down at the sheriff's department. Good luck with the awards ceremony." He opens the door and steps out, but his gaze still remains pinned on mine. "I'm open tomorrow night if you're up for it."

"I'll absolutely be up for it," I assure him.

Noah breaks out into his signature killer grin. "That's what I like to hear."

The door clicks softly behind him, and I turn slowly in the direction of Everett's home.

Noah is wrong. On occasion you *do* get to see your loved ones again—at least I do. I have a feeling I'll be seeing a heck of a lot more of Everett's lookalike phantasm than I ever wanted to.

One thing is for certain. I'm not letting Everett Baxter out of my sight tomorrow.

CHAPTER 2

*C*reating a bevy of pumpkin spice everything means running my skeleton crew—mostly on loan from the Honey Pot Diner next door—right down to the weary bone. And since I've been baking and moving nonstop for a week solid, I've enlisted Everett's help in getting the goods to the awards venue, which just so happens to be at the Evergreen Manor, an inn right here in Honey Hollow—the only competition to my mother's B&B.

"You really need a van, Lemon," Everett grunts as he lifts the final load of pumpkin pies and pumpkin cheesecakes onto the kitchen counter of the Evergreen. "A refrigerated one at that. It could have saved us three trips at least."

I take a moment to glare over at the dearly departed version of him just over his shoulder. I'm still not certain it's his father—although I'll go with it for now.

"A van costs money, and the bakery is just clearing the black each month. I'd have to save for at least a year. Unless, of course—"

A wicked grin blooms over his face. It's so rare I can't help but shed a smile myself, but by the time my lips curve in the right direction, his has evaporated.

"I know all about the contest in Ashford." He pats his hands together as we finish up the delivery. Everett looks dapper in a dark inky suit and burnt orange silk tie, a pumpkin-themed hue if ever there was one. "Noah told me about it. Are you entering?"

"So, the two of you talk about me when I'm not around?" I give a cheeky wink. "Yes, I'm entering. And the grand prize, as I'm sure you're well aware, is a cargo van equipped with refrigeration. A woman by the name of Crystal Mandrake wins just about every year. She owns a bakery called A Cake Above down in Ashford." I make a face at the thought. I've met Crystal before, and she's the queen of baking mean. "It's being held just a few days before Thanksgiving, and I know I'll be swamped, but I'm going to do it anyway."

"You bet you're going to do it. Even if I have to man that bakery myself. You really need a van. I wouldn't worry about Crystal Mandrake. I'm pretty sure you have it in the bag. Besides, were you really going to move all this food on your own? It would have taken three trips. Not to mention, cheesecake is heavy."

"Tell me about it." I iron out the front of my electric blue dress with my hands, and Everett gives an approving nod.

"You look good tonight, Lemon."

My eyes meet with his, and I can't help but note there's a sadness veiled in his gaze.

The spook behind him attempts to dip a finger into a pumpkin swirl cheesecake, and a breath hitches in my throat.

"Watch what you're doing," I hiss a little too curt, and Everett turns around to follow my gaze.

"I mean you." I spin him back my way, my fingers inadvertently digging into his steely muscles. Everett is so fit you'd think he lifted buildings each morning before he ran off to the courthouse.

"Whoa." He turns his head just enough as if he suspects something. "You're not looking at someone's long-lost pet, are you? And by lost, I mean dead."

"No." I shake my head up at this frightfully handsome

devil before me who just so happens to have a frightfully handsome doppelgänger following him wherever he goes. It's a terrifying thing, really. And I'm not quite sure how Everett would feel about it. My guess is, not good.

Everett frowns down at me. "Lemon, you called me to your place last night at ten o'clock asking if I'd brush your cat's hair."

I choke in response, unsure of which direction to take this. "Can you blame me? He's a long-haired cat. And look at you"—I motion up at those luscious black locks—"you are clearly good at men's hair."

"For a second, I thought you might be hitting on me." No smile. "But then you kept looking over my shoulder like you are now." He turns and gives a curt nod as if acknowledging the spectral between us. "And I think I recall a rather deranged yet hauntingly truthful conversation we had a few weeks back." His gaze softens as he looks to me. "Lemon, give it to me straight. What do you see? A cat, a dog? My mother ran a bona fide zoo. It could be anything."

My mouth opens, and just as I'm about to lob a big, fat, furry lie his way, Collette Jenner bounds in wearing a skin-tight red dress with ruching up and down the sides as if she stole the lining right out of a casket.

"Here you are," she trills while inspecting Everett as if he were a side of juicy beef before turning to me and smacking her lips with disgust. "Lottie, you wouldn't happen to have something for a headache, would you? I feel a humdinger coming on, and I'd rather die than throb with a migraine tonight."

"No, I don't. Sorry. I tend to travel with just my keys and wallet during deliveries. If I can't keep it in my pockets, I can't keep track of it. And after I lost the first three purses—"

"Okay, okay!" Her voice hikes to obnoxious decibels. "I asked for an aspirin, not a soliloquy." She turns to Everett. "I have very important people to introduce you to. Come, come." She snaps him up by the hand, and he does the same to me.

"You're coming for the ride, Lemon."

"I can't go out there." I free my hand from his. "I'm a part of the catering staff. I wasn't invited to the event."

"*I'm* inviting you."

Collette huffs my way. Her crimson hair is pulled back into a bun, and her makeup looks flawless with matching red lipstick. An entire stratum of granite colors is dusted over her eyelids.

"Be out there in five, Essex," she hisses at him before whirling right back out of the kitchen.

Essex. It seems all of Everett's exes have a propensity of calling him by his proper moniker, but since he prefers to go by Everett, I do as I'm told. I tend to follow orders—except when Noah and a dead body are involved, but that's another story.

"Go on, Everett. Get out there. You're acting as if you're afraid of Collette." I can't help but wrinkle my nose. Everyone in Honey Hollow is a little afraid of Collette.

He scowls at the thought. "I promise you I'm nowhere near afraid of that woman. I think she's seeing someone here, and she's brought me along to make him jealous. I don't like feeling as if I'm being manipulated."

"Manipulated? Or has your ego imploded?"

Everett growls as he takes ahold of my hand.

"What are you doing?"

"I'm about to introduce my date to the PR crowd on the other side of this wall."

"*I'm* your date?" Horror jolts through me at the thought. "Noah is not going to like this one bit."

"He won't mind," he says, breezing us out into the cool air of the dining hall where people move about, mingling and snapping up champagne glasses as if they were a requirement for survival. And on a night like this, they just might be. Jazz music plays softly from the speakers. The entire Evergreen Manor is decorated with fall leaves of every citrine color, pumpkins and wreaths made of cranberries. Across the room, I spot Naomi, Keelie's twin sister—but with that long black hair and sinister look on her face, you would never know they were related at all. Naomi runs the Evergreen Manor, so

I knew on an intrinsic level that the run-in was inevitable.

Everett leans in. "He can consider it payback. There was once a girl he borrowed from me. Only he wasn't as kind enough to return her."

Before I can ask all of the appropriate questions, we're standing in a circle with Collette and her glamorous co-workers while she gets to the punch line and the crowd breaks out into laughter.

"*Essex!*" Her face lights up at the sight of him and then falls just as fast once she sees he's holding my hand. "I'd like for you to meet my boss, Mr. Brad Rutherford." She motions to an older gentleman, handsome in a generic way, salt and pepper hair, dark serious eyes. He scans Everett as if he were a piece of furniture.

Mr. Rutherford offers Everett a nod of approval. "Nice to finally meet you. I was beginning to think you were the invisible man."

Another round of chortles circles the crowd as Collette's face turns hot pink with embarrassment.

"Of course, he's *real*, Brad. Why would I make up a big hunk of love like Essex?" She giggles at a stocky blonde, her hair too is in a chignon, an unflattering wrap dress peeling open at the leg. "Essex, this is Jenna Hatfield, my co-worker at the firm. She's my one true friend." She glances back to the girl. "But too bad for you, because Judge Baxter is one toy I'm not sharing. He's mine, all mine!"

More chortling ensues, and I can't help but roll my eyes. Little do these poor souls realize there's no actual toying around occurring between the two of them.

"Funny you should say that." A tall brunette with stick straight hair, complete with bangs that are a tad bit too short, and pouty lips that look as if she's spent the last thirty years sucking on a lemon huffs at the thought. She's pale with far too much kohl liner ringed around her eyes, and her lipstick is dragon's blood red. Everything about her gives off a Goth effect. "He's holding someone else's hand right now. It looks like you might not want to share, but he sure does."

The crowd breaks out into a violent burst of laughter, and Collette's flesh burns a deep shade of crimson that rivals her dress *and* her hair.

Poor Collette. It really must be bad if even I'm feeling sorry for her.

"Well, he *is* mine." She openly glares at Everett as if there will be hell to pay. And now I'm fearing for the good judge and his lack of good judgment for dragging me out here to witness the event. "May I have a word with you?" Collette hisses.

Before Everett can answer, she whisks him out the main doors to the ballroom, and the rest of the group turns to themselves and mingles.

The sickly-sweet scent of gardenia comes at me from behind. "What are *you* doing here?"

I turn to find none other than Naomi glowering at me as if I were ruining her night. Naomi used to have an insane crush on my high school boyfriend, Otis *Bear* Fisher, and she hasn't cared for me since.

"You know why I'm here. I brought the dessert."

"I mean here, *here*." She pulls me by the wrist and leads me to the door. "Catering staff belongs in the kitchen unless otherwise instructed. You're not to mix with the guests. These are very important people."

"I'm here with Everett," I say just to watch her squirm and squirm she does. Naomi, just like every other ovary-endowed woman in the Western Hemisphere, has one serious lustful hankering for Everett. "As his date."

She squirms twice as hard. "Wait a minute. Rumor has it, you tricked some poor goof into thinking he's your boyfriend—and I happen to know it's *not* Judge Baxter," she hisses out that last part like the threat it is.

Voices rise from the hall to my left, and I spot Collette tossing her arms in the air, red-faced and angry.

"Never you mind who my boyfriend is," I say, trying to push past this dark and twisted version of my bestie.

Naomi shoots a dark look toward the shouting. "Never you mind about Collette. She's just as annoying as you are. I hate her, too."

"Well, she may not be my favorite person either, but I'm not liking the sound of this argument." I take off before Naomi has a chance to protest.

"You can't have two men, Lottie! That's one over the limit. Keep your Fox and give the sexy man with a gavel to me," she calls out as I speed to the oversized doors, and the shouting grows louder.

A small crowd lingers at the edge of the cavernous hall where Everett and Collette seem to be going at it full steam.

"*Everett!*" I snatch him by the sleeve and drag him all the way to the kitchen. "It's time to serve the dessert."

And we do just that. Soon enough, the entire banquet room holds the scents of pumpkin spice, nutmeg, cloves, and a whole lot of cinnamon as the blooming crowd indulges in the pumpkin cheesecake, the pumpkin pie, pumpkin pinwheels, pumpkin rolls, pumpkin brownies, pumpkin sugar cookies, and let's not forget the pumpkin lattes in the fun pumpkin-shaped mugs.

I spot Collette speaking to the brunette that so freely humiliated her just a little while ago. Collette is a heck of a lot nicer than I am. That woman would have quickly become persona non-grata to me.

Collette tosses her hands, exasperated as their conversation grows more animated, and a crowd drifts between us.

"I'm getting the feeling Collette has a hard time holding onto friends."

"And you're going to lose one if you don't tell me the truth."

I turn to Everett and gasp. "Are you threatening me?" That spook behind him grows toweringly large for no good reason, and I swallow down a scream, petrified at the sight. My goodness, where is the waiter with a tray full of champagne when you need him?

"Yes. I mean no." He glances over his shoulder. "What are you looking at, for Pete's sake? Lemon—do you or don't you see a dead pet in my presence?"

My mouth opens and closes. I've never been a good liar... And then it hits me. I don't have to.

"No." I give a little shrug as Collette's boss charges past us, and we follow him with our eyes as he stalks off toward the exit. "He looks fit to be tied."

Everett cranes his neck through the crowd as he looks in that direction. "That woman Collette was speaking to is Jules King. She was up for the same award that will supposedly go to Collette tonight. I was briefed on all the inter-office drama last week."

"But why would that make *him* so angry?"

"I doubt it has anything to do with that woman. Collette has a way of giving every individual a reason to blow their top all on their own. In truth, I'm surprised his wife isn't stalking after her." He glances toward a demure brunette with shoulder-length hair, orange lips —and something about her reminds me a little of my mother. "It's a well-known fact Collette is seeing her husband."

My mouth falls open, and without thinking, my feet lead me in Collette-the-Homewrecker's direction as if I were about to give her a piece of my mind myself.

The sound of shouting ensues again, this time in a three-way match and, sure enough, there they are.

Jules King, the irate co-worker, gets in Collette's face and roars something out before heading off in the direction of the restrooms, leaving Collette and Mr. Rutherford going at it like seasoned pros.

Everett gently pulls me back into the ballroom.

"Ever hear the expression let sleeping dogs lie?"

"They're not sleeping."

"Then let howling cats roar." He nods toward the pumpkin pie. "Shall we?"

"We shall."

Soon enough, the ceremony officially gets underway, and Collette's boss, Mr. Rutherford, is on stage handing out fancy diamond-shaped awards as if they were Halloween candy. It begs the question, if everyone wins an award tonight, does it really mean all that much? Although, I must admit, it'd make a snazzy paperweight. I'm willing to bet that at least one person in the room would be willing to trade one of those sparklers for a whole pumpkin cheesecake, and I just so happen to have my bartering tool in the kitchen.

I'm sandwiched between Collette and Everett at the table and feel strangely as if Everett has morphed into a child during an ugly custody battle. To hear Collette threaten me, you'd think I were stopping her from seeing him on weekends *and* holidays.

"You're his ex," I whisper over to her in between her bouts of insanity. "The very definition begs to ask why he was kind enough to be here to begin with."

She grits a pressured laugh through clenched teeth. "If you'd scoot over a seat the way I asked, then we wouldn't be having an issue, Lottie Lemon," she says it all in a streamlined sentence without moving her lips. Collette is proving to be quite the ventriloquist. "But you never do as you're told, do you? I bet that boyfriend of yours has asked a dozen times for you not to see other men, and now look where you are? On a date with another man! My man to be exact." She reaches across from me and fondles Everett's hand. I can't help but avert my eyes. It was Everett who insisted I seat myself between them, and now I know why. She's a predator.

Mr. Rutherford calls Collette's name from the podium, and she quickly downs the rest of her pumpkin spice latte. She's boldly polished off a pumpkin spice cheesecake and a slice of my soon-to-be-famous pumpkin pie at Everett's suggestion. It's clear she'd eat a pound of mud to please Everett. Not that I'm comparing my delectable delights to the earthy mixture. But still. Collette is that dangerously eager to please.

A young man with dark hair and squared glasses applauds for her like mad. "Would you like me to escort you up there?" His voice rises in a peculiar manner as if the offer to trip her on the way up was an option. I'm quickly getting the idea Collette has no real friends. He stands and extends a hand toward her.

"No, Josh, you may never touch me." Her gaze drifts right back to Everett. "Excuse me, my love." She gives his hand a quick squeeze. "I'll be back with enough crystal to furnish that new house of yours." She glares over at the Goth brunette across from us. "Jules, if you'll excuse me, I'm off to accept the fruit of my labor."

Both Jules King and the demure brunette, aka Mrs. Rutherford, exchange a glance.

Hey? Maybe Collette invited Everett here to debunk any theories about her having an affair with her boss? In that case, Collette is right. My presence really didn't add anything to the situation.

Jules King leans in and leers at me. "That woman has my position and my award." She openly glares at me as if I were somehow an extension of Collette.

Jenna Hatfield, the blonde with the uncooperative wrap dress, leans my way. "Once Collette Jenner sets her mind to something, or someone"—she gives a covert glance Mrs. Rutherford's way—"it or they are more or less hers." She glances down at her untouched pumpkin pie as if she took this personally.

We turn to the stage where the spotlight makes Collette's chandelier earrings sparkle like mad, blinding the room with a spectral glow. Speaking of specters...

Oh my word. What is Everett's not-so friendly ghost doing looming behind Collette like some towering spook set out to frighten the entire room?

Collette leans in toward the mic, and her décolletage dips dramatically as those girls of hers threaten to make an appearance. My word, it's like she's actually harboring flesh-covered cantaloupes in there. I've never seen a pair so round and perky, not to mention the fact they look like they weigh ten pounds each easy. It must be a real killer.

"I'd like to thank everyone who came out to see me accept this award this evening." She extends a hand toward our table, and three of the women growl audibly. It's clear Collette is on better terms with the table than the women seated at it. "And a special thank you to the one man I simply cannot live without." She shoots a quick glance to her left at Mr. Rutherford, and her mouth opens wide but not a sound comes out. Her hand reaches for her throat as her affect morphs from prideful to frightful. A choking sound emits from her throat as she settles her mouth right over the mic as if she were about to swallow it.

"Poison," she says it lower than a whisper, but that haunting word reverberates around the room like a haunting echo.

Just like that—Collette falls to the floor in a heap, passed out cold. And judging by that blue hue that's quickly taking over her complexion, she won't be waking up anytime soon.

It looks to me as if Collette Jenner just dropped dead.

CHAPTER 3

"Poison?" The word circles the room on a demonic loop as Josh, the young man from our table—who was specifically instructed not to touch her, is currently administrating resuscitative efforts, mouth-to-mouth.

His ear moves over her heart, and a moment pulses by before he rises to his knees and announces, "She's dead!"

The room breaks out into gasps and screams as

dessert plates and mugs alike are violently pushed to the center of the table as if they were serpents.

Once, when I was twelve, I baked a lala berry pie for my mother's birthday party, and just as everyone indulged in their first delicious bite, a bevy of tiny worms made their presence known from inside the seemingly innocent berries. Up until now, that was my most cringe-worthy baking experience—but something tells me I may have inadvertently usurped myself.

Everett jumps on stage, along with Mr. Rutherford and just about every other man in the room as if their collective testosterone-laden efforts were needed to bring this damsel back from deathly distress.

Time seems to stand still and speed up all at once, and before we know it, the room is flooded with sheriff's deputies.

Naomi gives my arm a violent shove. "You killed her!"

A breath gets locked in my throat as the house lights go on and remove the fantasy-like aura from the room.

"No." The word pumps from me breathy and void of the proper conviction as every face in the vicinity turns my way.

Mr. Rutherford's wife takes ahold of the oversized mug Collette was last sipping from and sniffs it. "There's murder in this cup!"

"No!" I stand, taking a staggering step back. "Put that down," I hiss. "This is an active homicide investigation."

A dark murmur strums behind me as an all too familiar cologne permeates my senses. "You got that right."

Noah pops up beside me. "I'd like to ask everyone to head to the north lobby where deputies are waiting to get your information. Please do not panic. You are not in any kind of trouble. This is purely routine on behalf of the department. And we ask that you please file out in an orderly manner."

The entire room appears to evacuate at once, and instead of joining the herd, I wrap my arms around Noah. He's all decked out in a well-fitted suit, and I'm finding that stern expression of his vexingly sexy. I'm pretty certain that a bout of wild lust for my newly minted boyfriend is entirely unacceptable during a murder investigation in which the goods from my bakery are being implicated. But I can't help it. It's like some safety mechanism going off in my brain so I don't leap completely off sanity's edge.

A redheaded stunner stops short of where we're standing. "Detective Fox, you are here as a professional. Might I remind you this is not a booty call." She stalks off toward the stage while shouting orders at the medics.

"A *what*?" I laugh as I loosen my hold on him. The last

thing I want to do is get him thrown off the force before he's even begun. "Nobody says booty call anymore." I snarl over at Detective Fairbanks. I'm betting she's just jealous she's not the one getting booty from Noah. I don't need a road map to know where her affections lie. I saw the way she looked at him all last month while they worked on Hunter's murder investigation together. Suffice it to say, I was not impressed.

"She's right." Noah plucks a small notebook from his pocket. "Let's have it, Lot. What are your thoughts?"

"You want my thoughts?" I'm suddenly flattered and blushing—two things I might add, that are also most likely inappropriate to be feeling while there's a corpse less than twenty feet away.

"Yes." He bobs his head as if it were a given, those deep emerald eyes pinned hard over mine. "You have a keen sense of observation. And from what I gather, you were seated at the same table."

I quickly relay the events of the night, one by one—Collette's possessiveness over Everett, Everett's theory about her bringing him here to make someone jealous, the argument they had, her argument with Mr. Rutherford, the humiliation she endured, the best friend, the co-worker who insisted Collette took her job, and, of course, poor Josh, who Collette rejected, only to have him be the only one willing to administer oxygen when she needed it most.

"Okay, that's good." Noah hardly has a chance to look up when Ivy Fairbanks shoves her lips to his ear. He nods while giving me a sideways glance. "I see." She takes off again, and he's left sniffing the air as if girding himself for what comes next. "Just so you know, the sheriff's department is issuing a search warrant for both the bakery and your home." He blows out a heavy breath. "I'll have to take you down to Ashford for questioning, get your fingerprints on file, that sort of thing."

"Good grief."

Everett pops up, and I squint over at him as if assessing if he's the real deal or that ghost that's been haunting the vicinity. And how strange is it that Collette was the one that bit the big one?

I suck in a sharp breath. "Everett, did you eat the pie? My goodness, you could have poison coursing through your bloodstream right this minute!"

Noah balks, "Lottie, are you implicating yourself?"

"No." My hands wave wildly in his face. "I'm not, I swear. It's just that Collette's last word was *poison* and she was clutching her throat, so I just assumed that someone laced her food or drink and maybe somebody else's." Those last few words trail off as that handsome specter comes over with a blooming grin. "What do you want?" I hiss at him without meaning to.

Noah glances over his shoulder at the podium before

looking to me. "Lottie, what were you doing here at the table?"

Naomi pops up over my shoulder, and I jump. "I can answer that. She was on a *date*." She manufactures a wicked smirk at Everett. "And boy was Collette pissed to see it." She takes off after stirring the pot adequately to her liking. It's well past Halloween, but Naomi still wears her proverbial witch's hat loud and proud.

Noah's mouth opens as he looks from Everett to me. "You were his date?" He winces as if trying to process it all.

"I can explain."

Everett steps in close, and that suspicious look in his eyes doesn't bode well for me. "Who were you talking to just a moment ago?"

"I can explain that, too."

Noah hitches a thumb to the podium. "I'd better see what's going on up there." He takes off, and a cloud of grief weighs heavy on me.

Everett's chest expands a mile wide. "What's going on? Did you see one of those things—those *creatures* from the great beyond?" Everett looks both angry and remorseful that he needed to verbalize such a ludicrous thing. "Collette is dead, Lemon. Please, tell me right now if you somehow were able to predict this."

"No, I wasn't." That ghost of his glowers over at me as if he were angry to be here. "It's not my fault. Maybe

Collette didn't have pets?" I whisper in hopes not a living soul in the room hears this asinine conversation.

Everett straightens. "You saw a *person*?"

"How did you know?"

"Law of deduction." He shuffles us to the side of the ballroom. "Who was she?"

"It was a *he* and I don't know exactly, but I have a pretty good idea."

A heavy sigh expires from him as he considers this. "Maybe it was her father or a grandfather?"

"Or maybe it was *your* father?" I shrink a little as I say it. "You wouldn't happen to have a picture of him on your phone, would you?" The lookalike specter walks up and stands shoulder to shoulder with Everett, and their resemblance is uncanny. "Never mind. I don't think I'll need it."

Everett leans in, his eyes narrowed over mine. "Did you say my *father*?"

"That's right. I can't be a hundred percent certain, but I'd bet a soul or two."

The wily specter gives a barely-there wink, and I gasp.

"It is him!"

"*Geez*," Everett exhales in exasperation and pinches his eyes shut.

"I'm sorry." No sooner do I land my arm over him than I spot Noah's eyes popping in this direction, so I pull my arm right back as if snatching it from a fire. "It must be very hard to hear that. I don't know what's going on. This is certainly breaking protocol with everything I've ever known, which wasn't much to begin with."

He glares at the air around him for a moment. "You can tell my father to go away. I don't want him here."

My mouth falls open as I look to the seemingly unmoved poltergeist amongst us. "I'm sure he heard, but nonetheless he's not going anywhere."

"Then I will." Everett takes off for the hall, leaving me standing there staring at his ghost of a father.

"You heard him." I try to shoo him away with my hands. "You're not going anywhere, are you?"

He shakes his head, slow and serious. Dear Lord, he's just as ornery as his son.

"Is Everett in danger?"

He studies my features, one inch at a time, as if there would be a quiz on them later. Not one spooky visitor from the other side has ever spoken to me—and for the most part, I'm thrilled about it, considering the fact I learned in Sunday school that mediums were heavily frowned upon at Honey Hollow's Covenant Church. And then an idea hits me. We could play a quick game of charades, and I could guess what his mission might be. That's totally different than communicating with the dead—oh, wait…

"Look"—I sigh just as heavy as his son did—"I don't know what you want, but your son didn't die today. Someone else did." I turn a bit so that I'm facing the wall in the event Ivy Fairbanks spots me chatting away with myself and escorts me straight to the psych ward. "If you have unfinished business with your son, I'm afraid I can't help you with that. I'm no expert in living relationships let alone ones that are well past their prime."

He glowers at me, and those eyes of his beacon out bright as warning signals. He lifts his arm and points hard my way before pointing to himself, then in the direction Everett took off in. And just like that, he evaporates.

A tiny whimper escapes me. It's unnerving enough when an animal pulls a disappearing act like that let alone a once-upon-a-human.

Me, him, and Everett.

I wonder what that means?

Something tells me I'm about to find out.

CHAPTER 4

*N*oah Fox presses his hooded gaze to mine, those hypnotic marbled eyes taking me in as if we were about to indulge in a feast of flesh.

"Right hand," he says, helping me hold my fingers over the small device that lights up neon green as it captures my prints. "Thumb." I'm quick to comply, and we do the left hand, too.

The Ashford County Sheriff's Department is a boxy white building with white linoleum floors, plain black desks, a few cubicles, a few mysterious halls, and a holding tank somewhere in the back.

"So, am I getting thrown in the pokey?" I can't help but take a stab at humor. Although, I'm not laughing, and I don't suspect I will be for some time to come. Just because I didn't see eye to eye with Collette doesn't mean I wanted her dead. Come to think of it, I probably should have said that out loud.

"Don't worry." Noah pulls my hand forward and lands a kiss on my fingertip. "Nobody thinks you're guilty."

"Except for the people who think I did it." I hold my phone up for him to see. "This is a picture Keelie sent me. Apparently, the bakery is under siege. Dozens of sheriff's deputies are currently sweeping through the place, and word on the street is they plan on being there well into the morning."

"I'm sorry." He glances past me. "Look, you answered all the questions we had for you. And we now have your fingerprints on file. How about I give you a ride home?" His lids hood slightly once again, and my heart thumps hard against my chest. Noah Fox is a ball of testosterone, and he can't help but permeate the vicinity with it.

"It sounds perfect. I'd love nothing more than to spend some serious alone time with you."

An icy breeze slices through my clothes as Ivy Fairbanks whisks into the room and hastily takes off her jacket.

"I'm glad you're here, Fox. I've got an entire list of suspects we need to comb through. Starting with"—she spins on her heel and stops short when she spots me— "Carlotta Lemon."

"It's Lottie, please. Nobody calls me that." There is not a person in my life who refers to me as Carlotta. I've been Lottie since the day I landed in the Lemons' arms. "Carlotta is more or less a formality."

She folds her arms across her chest, that smug look riding high on her perfect little face. "And these are formal circumstances." She looks to Noah. "Has she undergone questioning and been fingerprinted?"

"Yes and yes." He winces my way because we both know what's coming next.

"Then she's free to go. You, however, are not. We need to sift through the suspect list. Our chances of catching the killer is best within—"

"The first twenty-four hours," Noah finishes for her. "I know."

"I can help," I gladly volunteer. "I mean, I was there. I heard and saw everything."

"No." Ivy doesn't even bother to look up at me. "The last thing we need is a civilian tainting the case. So, unless you have a confession ready to bubble out of you, I suggest you leave the premises."

My mouth falls open. "*Confession?*" I practically mouth the word to Noah as he walks me to the door. "But you're my ride. I'll wait out in the hall. Besides, I need some of those soothing kisses you dole out if I'm ever going to fall asleep tonight," I whisper that last part.

"I heard that," Ivy chimes as she continues to busy herself with paperwork. I bet it's all fake. Who works with paper anymore? The entire department has crossed over to software and computers. It's like she's living in the Stone Age.

Noah presses out a warm smile. "I'll arrange for a car to take you home."

"An official sheriff's car? No way. Word will spread around town, and they'll have me in stocks by noon. The people of Honey Hollow do not play games. The last thing I need is to be paraded around town in the back of a cruiser. It's bad enough the boys in blue are pilfering the bakery. I'll have to toss out half my stock just to rid it of their germs." I run my fingers down his tie and look up at this gorgeous man before me. "I'll wait."

His dimples ignite with a grimace. "No can do. This could take hours, and I'd never want to steal a moment of sleep from you. Can you call someone?"

"To come all the way to Ashford?"

Noah tips his head with a look of remorse. "Everett will do it."

"No way. No thank you." Just the thought of Everett

and his unhappy haunting makes me want to shudder. "I know just the person to call."

"Great." He presses a warm kiss over my lips, just enough to keep me wanting more. "Remember, Lot, stay out of my investigation. I need you safe."

I tip my head back and withhold the urge to snarl. "Will do." I head out of the station and into the night.

Keelie absolutely refused to drive to Ashford. *Refused* to pick up her very best friend. Although, in her defense, she did say she was close to getting a number from an exceptionally adorable sheriff's deputy. It's nice to know I come first except when I don't. I'd call Lainey, but I know for a fact she'll be getting up in three short hours. She's always been an early riser—and she's also the head of the Honey Hollow Library, where I happen to know she works a shift tomorrow. My mother would die a thousand deaths if I asked her to pick me up at the sheriff's department. So that just leaves one person.

Otis *Bear* Fisher rolls up in his beat-up truck with a magnetic sign slapped to the side reading *Fisher Construction. Repairs, Additions, and More!*

"What's up, Lot?" He nods as I get in and buckle up. Bear is my ex and for good reason. Sure, he's a gorgeous fair-haired surfer type—without a single wave to hit in the great state of Vermont—but he cheated on me something awful, and it's an experience I never want to repeat.

Columbia—and what I lovingly refer to as the New York debacle—runs through my mind, and I let it run right back out. Lord knows I don't have time to ruminate on how all of my exes have done me wrong. Especially not while Noah is trapped in that *Ivy* tower. I'm sure she was counting the seconds until she was alone with him just to hogtie him with those long red tendrils of hers.

"So, did they throw the book at you?" He chuckles as we head onto the highway.

"Very funny. You know I didn't kill Collette."

He shakes his head wistfully. "It's Hunter all over again. I'd worry about a serial killer, but thankfully Stella got put away." Stella Morgan was the stripper who happened to have Hunter's baby and then killed poor Hunter as a means to keep him from his child. I'm just glad she's getting the help she needs. "I can't believe Collette's dead. I'm in the middle of replacing her water heater. I still need to get some of my tools out of her house."

"How are you going to do that?"

"I've got a key." A sly smile rides over his face as he gives a slight chuckle into the road.

"Why are you laughing? Oh my goodness!" It hits me like a ton of pornographic bricks. "You were with Collette, weren't you?"

"Long after we were through. Besides, that's been

over for a while. But yeah, she gave me a key. Said I could come over whenever I wanted."

"Whenever you wanted?" Something quasi-illegal is brewing within me. I can feel it. "So, the neighbors are used to seeing you walk in and out of her home?" A rush of adrenaline kicks in right along with what I'm guessing is a very bad idea.

"That's right. And no, I'm not taking you. I'm sure the sheriffs will have that place on lockdown come morning."

"True. But they're sort of busy at the bakery at the moment." I glance over to Bear and shrug as he looks my way.

"Oh no."

"Oh yes. They'll be there in just a few hours. You said so yourself. We'll be in and out, I promise."

"What?" He wheezes as he leans toward the wheel. "What in the heck are you looking for?"

"I don't know. But I do know that someone is setting me up, and I need to get to the bottom of this before things escalate. Maybe she left a note, a to-do list, or maybe she has a casserole she forgot in the oven, and I can turn it off before the entire place burns down."

"First, we both know Collette has never eaten a casserole let alone baked one. Second, every last list she ever wrote was on her phone, and I'm pretty sure she had it with her tonight."

"Fine." I fold my arms over my chest in a fit of desperation. "Then I'll just help you pick up your tools and we'll leave. Once they have that place under quarantine, it might be weeks before you see them again." He starts to say something, and I hold up a finger. "Do not argue with me, Bear Fisher. In the event you've forgotten, I helped track down Hunter's killer. You owe me."

"Fine. But if I get arrested for breaking and entering—"

"It's not breaking and entering if you have a key." I hope.

"Let's just say I'm not opposed to throwing you under the bus if we're caught."

"We never were much of a team to begin with."

COLLETTE JENNER LIVES in a densely populated neighborhood filled with professionals who regularly commute to Ashford. A few years back, Honey Hollow was pegged as a desirable bedroom community for those looking to reduce their housing costs. But what they save in housing they lose in gas. Ashford is still a decent ride away.

The streetlamp above Collette's tiny Tudor blinks on and off every few seconds, giving the neighborhood a haunted appeal. Her house is shrouded with mist, the walkway damp and slippery as Bear leads us around back and lets us in through a door that opens into the kitchen. He flicks on the lights, and my stomach explodes in a vat of acid.

"What did you do that for?" I bat my hand at him.

"Because if we walk around with flashlights, I'm pretty sure that suggests we're doing something wrong. I'm just here to get my tools, remember?"

"Oh right," I say, casting a quick glance around. Her cabinets are bone white, and the counter has a dark green slab of granite sitting over it. It looks staged, cold and sterile, like a showroom you might see at a hardware store. There's not one sign of human occupation in sight, and I can't say I'm too surprised. "I'll be right back."

"Lot?" Bear calls after me. "I'm getting my tools!"

"You do that." I quickly make my way into the living room. Not a pillow out of place, and the fireplace looks as if it's never been used. It's immaculately decorated with rustic furniture, clean lines, and leather sofas. No sign of a desk or even a briefcase near the door. I head down the hall, two spare bedrooms that look as if they were plucked out of a Pottery Barn catalog.

I head upstairs, and the trail of her perfume still lingers in the air. A pang of grief hits me because I know for a fact she'll never be back in this house again. I turn on the hallway light with my sleeve and head into the master bedroom. A large king-sized bed takes up most of the space along with a headboard that stands at least six feet tall that leans against the wall. Her briefcase sits opened on a desk near her bed. I quickly shuffle my way over and turn on the flashlight on my phone to get a better look at it.

Flowery handwriting decorates a yellow legal pad, and I quickly snap a picture. Something about deductions. The name Jules is crossed out, and the words *CALL BRAD* are all in caps.

I move over to the side of the bed and open up the nightstand with the sleeve of my dress. No sooner do I flash the light over the contents than I suck in a sharp breath.

A whip, a rope, a ball gag, and a pair of handcuffs stare back at me looking guilty as sin, and I choke while ogling the goods.

"*Collette Jenner*," I whisper as I carefully close it up again. I head into her bathroom and flash the light over the counter, exposing a basket full of cosmetics, a brush filled with red hair, and next to it sits a small orange Post-it with the words *Jungle Room* scrawled hastily followed by an exclamation point and a severe slash underneath it as if highlighting its importance.

"*Lot?*" Bear calls from below. "Time to head out."

I take a quick picture, turn off the light, and head back down.

Bear picks up his tool bag and sags my way as if he were sorry he ever met me, and that might be true. "You find what you were looking for?"

"I wasn't looking for anything, so I guess the answer is no. Hey, was Collette into kink?"

Bear's eyes widen a notch as he leads me out the door and locks up behind us.

"So, you found the toys, did you?" A perverse laugh strums from his chest.

"Oh gross. You are disgusting."

Bear drives me home, and all the way there I picture Collette wrapped up and strapped up, but it's not Bear I envision hopping around on that mattress with her—it's Everett.

"Thanks for the ride," I say, piling out and securing my purse over my shoulder. "How about we keep our last stop a secret just between you and me?"

His cheek flickers as he stares up at me. "Fine. But now we're even. My family has been through enough grief this last month. The last thing I need to do is get in over my head in another murder investigation."

Noah's reprimand comes back to me. "We did not investigate," I say as I wave him off and turn toward my brand new rental.

Next door the lights are on, and I note a silhouette in

the bedroom window upstairs as well as one in the living room, and both of those familiar frames just so happen to be looking my way. I give a brief wave and head inside my own home and seal the door shut behind me.

Collette Jenner is dead, both the bakery and I are under suspicion, Everett has a ghost attached to his side that is far more ornery than he is, and I might have stepped into Noah's investigation in a roundabout way.

And here I thought November was going to be all about baking a cornucopia of cookies and getting ready for the Thanksgiving Pumpkin Pie Bake-Off. I can think of very few things I'm grateful for at the moment.

Pancake struts my way, sleepy eyed and overall grumpy looking.

"Come here, my sweet cat." I scoop him into my arms and press a gentle kiss over his forehead. "I'm thankful for you. Yes, I am." I rock him in my arms as I look out my window and over to Everett's home, now devoid of any light.

"I bet he was all too familiar with Collette's freaky side." I frown openly at the dark expanse outside my window. "I sure didn't know Collette. I guess you can't really know someone, know their deep, dark secrets, what devices and toys they have lining their nightstand. I am curious about the Jungle Room, though. It sounded important, like she was excited about it."

I glance out into the cold, steely night as the fog rolls into the streets like a band of marching poltergeists.

I am staying out of Noah's investigation. But that doesn't mean I can't start my own. And the first clue I need to detangle is the mysterious Jungle Room.

What kinds of things might happen there?

I'm betting they're all very, very bad.

CHAPTER 5

*I*t's not until Tuesday that I'm able to reopen the bakery, and no sooner do I unlock the front door than a floodgate of tourists and morning commuters charge in. It didn't take me long to realize that fresh baked cinnamon rolls and fresh brewed coffee acted as a siren song to those wandering up and down Main Street. The cinnamon rolls were gone in a flash, but I still have plenty of fresh croissants, apple turnovers, and red velvet French toast—which I am personally obsessed with. Honestly, sometimes I think I make most of the treats to please my own palate.

By ten in the morning, my feet feel as if they'd voluntarily fall off if they could, my back aches, and my head is throbbing just begging for another cup of quick and dirty caffeination. I'd love nothing more than to fall into one of those pastel chairs Bear hand painted for me. Well, not for me per se, but the Cutie Pie Bakery and Cakery. With its butter yellow walls and nonpareil-colored mismatched furniture, the straggling oak limbs that stretch from the Honey Pot Diner next door and expand all across the ceiling of the café portion of this place, not to mention the fact each branch is wrapped in twinkle lights—this place holds a very real magic all its own. It was Bear's idea to blow a hole in the wall and create a walkway from the Honey Pot to the bakery—and it's safe to say it was his brightest idea yet.

Mom's travel club is just finishing up a meeting in the café, and I shuddered listening in on their enthusiastic conversations about visiting Manhattan in early December. Sure, the store windows are decorated like no other, there is typically a blanket of fresh fallen snow making the entire city feel like the inside of some magical snow globe, and the shopping—well, that's to die for year-round—but my own memories of the years I spent living in the city, my college years and a little just beyond that, were fraught with horrific memories. I loved my roommate. I loved my boyfriend, Curt, who quickly became my fiancé. But then, I came home a little early one afternoon and found them loving one another quite aggressively and loud as a fire alarm. I thought my roommate was getting her head sliced off from the sound of it. And to be honest, for a brief moment, I thought she was being accosted, which had me fully ready to slice off a few body parts of her would-be assailant—but as soon as I saw my soon-to-be ex, I high-tailed it out of there, out of the city, and straight back to Honey Hollow. It's almost ironic how I let Bear's indiscretions chase me out of Honey Hollow and Curt's chase me right back in.

The door to the Cutie Pie chimes and in walks Lainey looking every bit the fall princess in a burnt orange coat and matching lipstick. Lainey is gorgeous, and sweet, and I love her all the more now that we're no longer roommates ourselves. We almost killed one another growing up. Especially when someone borrowed someone else's sweater without asking. It was a three-way civil war among Lainey, our sister Meg, and me. Although, this last experiment in cohabitation seemed to go much smoother than the last.

"You're looking good today. Is there a special event at the library?"

Her tiny comma-like dimples press in. "We're hosting a field trip for Honey Hollow Elementary at one. We're calling it the Cornucopia of Books Festival. I've spent all morning pulling out every book in the children's section that might actually have a fall theme. Do you realize there is a serious shortage of books with fall themes? All I could find were a dozen board books. Oh well. Variety is the spice of life. That's my story, and I'm sticking to it."

"Do what you can with the Thanksgiving theme, but I'd show off the Christmas books as well."

Her light coffee-colored eyes light up. "That's a great idea! Thanksgiving is Christmas' underappreciated cousin anyway. That's all any store in town has been pushing since September. It's like Halloween jumps straight to Christmas—and, oh yeah, let's eat a turkey in November to strategize our Black Friday plans."

I slide a chocolate-filled croissant her way, and she hums with glee.

"There are definite benefits to having a sister who's a baker." She gives a cheeky wink as she deposits money into the tip jar. Lainey tips regularly because she knows I won't charge her for a thing. "So, how's the investigation going?" She makes a face as she takes a bite, and her affect is quickly restored.

"I'm not sure. Noah has been so busy we haven't had a second alone together."

"Sorry to hear it. Tanner took me to the movies last

night, and we ran into Forest. It's like no matter where I go, there he is."

"That's because you're meant to be together. You and Forest—not you and Tanner." Lainey dated Forest Donovan for as long as I can remember, and the two of them called it quits last summer over some silly dispute. And to make things even sillier, Lainey had the bright idea to land Tanner Redwood by her side in an effort to make Forest jealous. Everyone knows Tanner is a notorious playboy. Even Lainey knows that. But she doesn't care. There's a man to be made jealous and, by goodness, she'll stoop as low as needed to get the job done—all the way to the movies apparently.

Mom and her good friend, Eve Hollister, step up to the counter.

Eve twirls into her green wool coat. That emerald color reminds me of Noah's eyes, and I miss him all the more.

"Thank you for letting us linger, Lottie." Eve presses out a pleasant grin. My mother once told me that she and Eve were the same age, but it's hard to believe. Eve looks every bit your typical granny with white permed hair, heavily etched face full of soft wrinkles, and a judgmental disposition in general about life. She's been widowed for a while, has three kids who never visit, and has undergone every renovation known to man at that mansion of hers that sits like the odd man out at the edge of town.

Mom, in contrast, is fit for her age, her arms are well-toned, her hair cut to her shoulders in a wavy blonde bob, not a gray hair in sight thanks to her weekly trips to the Shear Beauty Salon, and she happens to have a penchant for dressing young and acting that way, too. My mother has been my role model for as long as I can remember, and I certainly hope I have her vitality and zest for life when I'm her age. Not to mention the fact she too has been a widow for years.

Eve leans in. "You're welcome to join us next month in Manhattan. Your mother says no one gives a tour quite like you."

"No thank you." I shoot a look to my mother. That woman knows I'd rather chop off both hands than head anywhere near the city. "But with my mother as a guide, I'm sure you'll have a good time."

"Of course, we will." She nods to my mother, forlorn. "Jackie Jenner, Collette's mother, was supposed to lead the group. Who would have thought that such a tragedy could have struck someone so young at that? *Poisoned!*" Eve bellows, and half the patrons look my way.

"Well, she wasn't poisoned by me. The bakery received the all clear." I haven't officially yet, but there are some details that simply aren't needed.

Mom pats my hand. "That's right, dear. You're innocent until proven guilty. That's how our country works."

"I won't be proven guilty. I didn't do a thing wrong."

Eve lifts a finger as she turns to go. "Anyhow, the funeral is Saturday, and I don't have a thing to wear. Funerals in Honey Hollow are becoming quite the social events. I'll see you girls there!" She gives a cheery wave as she speeds out the door.

Lainey makes a face. "I hate funerals. Hey? Do you think we've got a serial killer on the loose? I mean, three deaths in three months. Maybe those other people you caught were the wrong people!"

"*Stop*," I hiss. "Customers are leaving." I nod to a crowd ambling their way to the door. "See what you did? Nobody wants a little conversation about a serial killer with their morning pie."

"Speaking of pies." Mom rubs her hands together in anticipation, and my stomach sinks because I know where this is going. "Tell me when and where they're hosting that pumpkin pie contest in Ashford. I plan on being there with bells on. I heard last year they had a panel of ten judges. Six were male and three were widowers!" Her shoulders do that annoying shimmy thing that makes my stomach turn. Rumor has it that three-time winner Crystal Mandrake not only won the prize last year but she won a husband right off the judging panel as well. So I guess my mother isn't all that far off.

"Hey, wait a minute." I pick up the carafe and pour her a fresh cup of coffee. "What happened to Wallace Chad, the man with two first names? Don't tell me you've given him his walking papers already."

Mom waves him off as she takes a careful sip of her coffee.

"You didn't hear?" Lainey scoots in with an undeniable excitement tittering in her voice. "He got a job in Leeds working for a certain questionable financial institution."

I slap my hand over my mouth in shock. "No!" I told Mom and Lainey all about my adventures at the Martinelle Finance department where Everett and I posed as a couple last month to try to catch Hunter's killer. And, believe it or not, they offered a vital clue in the investigation. "He'll be in prison before you can say Thanksgiving dinner. I happened to know for a fact they're being investigated. But don't say a word." I slip my finger over my mouth.

Lily Swanson swoops in and grabs a couple of brownies out of the case. "Don't say a word about what?" She lifts a villainous brow. Come to think of it, everything about Lily is villainous. She's Naomi Turner's best friend for starters, and one is just as wicked as the other. But since I'm still short on a crew of my own,

Keelie who does all the hiring for the Honey Pot Diner next door, and now the bakery as well, brought her onboard to help out. As much as I hate to admit it, she does have a way with moving people through the line at lightning speed. She's been a real godsend.

"About the contest—" My mouth opens as I look to Lainey for help, but she just shrugs over at me while stuffing the rest of that croissant into her mouth. "I may not be eligible to participate in the bake-off." I glower at Lily a moment for making me confess it in front of her of all people. "But if you want to keep your job, I'd keep that little bit of info close to the vest. I still have a healthy order of Thanksgiving Day pies coming in on the regular."

Her little pink mouth rounds out. Lily is a dark-haired, honey-skinned stunner who has made no secret about her crush on Everett. "It's because of the poisoning, isn't it?"

I frown over at my mother. She and Lily have been vying for top spot on the gossip food chain for a while now, and here I am about to feed the frenzy.

"Yes," I say reluctantly. "But it has nothing to do with the bakery, so don't go chasing any of my customers away just yet."

Lainey cringes. "Is it because you're being investigated?"

I nod just as another crowd waddles through the

door, and a few golden maple leaves blow in right along with them. Fall in Honey Hollow is all about the magical show the leaves put on.

Lily takes off to help them out, and I pull out a pumpkin pinwheel cookie and take an angry bite.

Mom shakes her head at the thought. "Don't you worry. Once you're in the clear, they'll have to accept you. You already filled out the application long before the deadline. This will all work out in the end, and you'll be the owner of a brand new van for the bakery in no time!"

"From your mouth to—"

"Meg's ears!" Lainey's phone blares a happy little song, and she holds up the screen where Meg glares back at us with her over-dyed black hair and neon yellow contacts, her blue nails exposed as she flashes a peace sign.

Lainey picks up, and we FaceTime with our younger sister. Lainey fills her in on all the happenings at the library, and Mom regales us all with the tale of how she dumped Wallace—embellished as it were, it still brings me joy.

Meg peers over at me. "And what about you, Lottie? Trip over any more dead bodies?" She chortles into her latte. Her hair is pulled back into a messy bun, and yet she still manages to achieve supermodel status. Meg is a stunner when she's not trying to break anyone's back on the female wrestling circuit in Las Vegas.

Lainey and I groan in unison as our mother quickly rattles off all the gory details.

Meg's jaw unhinges, and it looks quite literal. "And she just dropped dead right there at the ceremony? After clutching her throat and screaming she was poisoned?" She looks over at me. "You're my new hero, Lot." She bursts out laughing. "Not only do you find the bodies but you're giving the morgue a fresh supply!" Tears are actually spouting from the corners of her eyes.

"Oh stop." Mom holds up a finger, her very real threat whenever we FaceTime. Our mother is not afraid to shut us down by way of that looming red button.

The door jingles and in walks a tall, handsome detective whom I might need to investigate to see if his pucker is still working. I haven't had a single kiss since Saturday.

"Noah!" I wave him over, and he's slow to break into a smile, which only makes him all the more comely. Noah has the body of a football player, and he's chosen to cover it with the suit of a well-dressed mobster. Noah is a god among us that accidentally escaped Olympus. Just having him in the bakery has caused every ovary in the vicinity to pop.

His dimples press in as he nods to the three of us. "Ladies."

I turn Lainey's phone in his direction. "Say hello to my sister, Meg. She's the wrestler in Las Vegas."

A genuine, warm smile graces his face and those adorable dimples dig in, and he looks every bit as scrumptious as those praline pumpkin bars I whipped up this morning.

"Nice to finally meet you, Meg. You have an amazing family."

"Oh, I know it." Meg's voice chirps from the tiny device. "So, what exactly are your intentions with my sister? If you even think about breaking her heart, I'll be moved to hop on the next plane and bust a rib. Believe you me, I know how to inflict maximum pain in all situations."

"Okay," Lainey says as she pulls the phone back. "And on that note, I have a library to tend to. My break was over fifteen minutes ago."

We say a quick goodbye to both Lainey and Meg just as Mom puts on her coat.

"I'll see you kids soon. I'm meeting the plumber in ten minutes."

Noah lifts his chin her way. "Trouble at the B&B?"

"There's always trouble at the B&B," she assures him just before squeezing his cheeks together with her hand. "Don't you worry about Meg and her mean threats, mister. Everyone knows you're a kind soul who would never break my daughter's heart." She speeds to the door, and her affect falls flat as she looks back at him. "But the threat is real if it has to be."

"I will make note of that."

The door closes behind her, and I can't help but cringe at Noah. "I'm sorry. And she's right. You're the kindest soul on the planet. Coffee and a cranberry scone?"

Any trace of a smile he had for my mother glides right off his face.

"I'm not feeling so kind, Lottie." Those serious eyes narrow in on mine. "I just found out there was a potential break-in at Collette Jenner's house the night she was murdered. You wouldn't happen to know anything about that, would you?"

I suck in a quick breath. Noah is either going to arrest me or break up with me for good. *Both* if I'm very unlucky, and Lord knows I have been extremely unlucky for a very long time.

A couple of customers turn this way and pick up on the tension, expecting a show, I'm sure.

"Would you like to take a walk, detective?"

Noah gives the hint of a nod. "And you are going to tell me everything."

CHAPTER 6

*N*ever offer a man a cranberry scone when you know his favorite treat in the world is a fresh baked chocolate chip cookie.

Noah and I step out into the crisp autumn air. The sky is veiled with dark clouds, and the streets are lined with crimson, gold, and bright orange leaves as if a ticker tape parade went through town and we forgot to clean up the mess.

"*Mmm.*" Noah moans his way through another

chocolate chip cookie and nods approvingly. I wised up quickly and threw a half dozen into a bag on our way out the door. Lily said she'd hold down the fort, but if I wasn't back by noon, she threatened to walk off the job. That's been her favorite threat to wield ever since she started. But Lily doesn't have to worry. I don't ever plan on leaving the bakery in her hands for too long.

"Truce?" I ask as he wolfs down another bite.

"Truce." He rolls the bag closed and picks up my hand as we make our way toward the enormous stone fountain in the town square. The park surrounding it is decorated with enough pumpkins to bake all of North America a pumpkin pie, not that anyone would eat it coming from me. And there's an oversized scarecrow staked into the center of the sprawling lawn where currently a line of tourists wait patiently to take a selfie with it.

Noah and I pause just past the fountain under the semi-covering of the town's hundred-year oak tree that we affectionately refer to as Nelson. Nell once said that this one inspired the oak in the Honey Pot Diner.

"Lottie"—his tone is sharp but tender, a true feat considering the contrast—"tell me that you didn't break into Collette Jenner's house the night she was murdered. Neighbors reported seeing Bear's truck there at eleven thirty. That puts it at about the same time he drove you home."

"How do you know Bear drove me home?"

His lips twitch just enough to make my insides melt. I've been craving them, and if I stare too long, I'm sure my mouth will water.

"Because you just admitted it."

"Ugh." I tip my head back in exasperation. "So not fair. Please do not use your ninja detective tactics on me." I look up at him pleadingly. "I'm your girlfriend, remember?"

His chest rumbles with a warm laugh as he pulls me in with the hook of his arm. "Yes, Lottie, you are. And I care about you more than anyone in the world. That's exactly why I don't want to see you getting mixed up in something you're already way too involved with."

"I'm sorry." It comes out curt because I'm really not at all. "But my bakery was being pilfered, and fingers were pointing in my direction before I ever left the Evergreen Manor that night. Bear's not in trouble, is he? He's my friend. Please go easy on him." Bear and I haven't always been on speaking terms, but after that horrible tragedy with Hunter, we've pretty much put our unsettled past behind us and have been nothing but amicable ever since. It's sort of nice having Bear as a friend.

Noah tips his head suspiciously. "You and Bear are friends again?"

"Yes. He's good with a hammer and happened to

have the key to Collette Jenner's house. He's the best kind of friend," I tease. "Not to mention after that nightmare with Hunter, we've put all past grievances aside."

"Good. I'm glad to hear that. But I'm not glad to hear that the two of you went into Collette's home after she was murdered." His eyes sharpen over mine. "What were you doing, and what did you find? Detective Fairbanks questioned him this morning, and the only reason you're not in Ashford sitting in the hot seat is because Bear emphatically denied having anyone with him. You do realize he perjured himself for you."

My hand flies to my lips. "Oh no, this is turning into another horrible nightmare. You can't tell Ivy. She'll ruin everything."

His eyes spin wild like pinwheels. "Lottie, you are crossing every line I'm asking you not to go near."

"You never instructed me not to go into that house." My voice hikes up a notch.

"Because common sense leads me to believe I wouldn't have to!" His voice matches mine, and a couple of tourists glance our way. "Look"—his voice softens as he brushes a kiss over my nose—"you are in way over your head. And I am not going to implicate you, but Fairbanks is smart enough to put two and two together. There was a streetlight malfunctioning in front of Collette's house, and half the neighborhood was up cursing at it when they saw Bear and a woman, with your height and hair coloring, ducking in through the back door. What happened when you got into the house?"

"Bear had been doing some work for her and needed to get his tools."

"At that time of night? Knowing what he did about her?" He lifts a brow.

"Okay, fine. I may have charmingly reminded him he owed me one—and he let me do my thing while he cleaned up his mess."

"Geez." He closes his eyes. "Did you touch anything?"

I shake my head. "I used my sleeve." I wince, and poor Noah shakes his head in disbelief.

"You're a seasoned pro. What did you see?"

"Nothing really. The house hardly looked lived in. I guess that's because she was always at the office. But I did find this." I take out my phone and pull up a picture of the notebook.

"*Crap!*" Noah looks as if he's about to jump out of his skin. "You took pictures? You need to delete those right now."

"No way." I pull my phone close to my chest. "There are some serious clues here. I just have to mine them a bit to see what they mean." I show him the legal pad filled to the brim with odd details she needed to tend to and the orange sticky note that reads *Jungle Room* enthusiastically. "And it turns out that good old Collette had a hankering for the dirty side of bedroom business." I blush a little when I say it. As much as I hate to admit it, I gave my virginity to Bear at a discounted rate in exchange for a bad pick-up line and a strong margarita. I gave much more to Curt, and I regret every mattress move I ever shared with him. I swore to myself I wouldn't let another man have me until I was certain he was the one. And my quivering thighs, my hungry to have him stomach, screams that Noah Corbin Fox is indeed the one.

"Dirty bedroom business?" His lids hang heavy as he whispers the words hot over my lips. "What did you see, Lottie?"

"She had these—I don't know, tools or toys in the nightstand next to her bed. Needless to say, I didn't take a picture of them. But they were out there."

"They weren't out there. You were snooping."

"Well, they may as well have punched my face as soon as I opened the drawer—with my sleeve."

"I'm sure Collette would have loved to have seen them do just that. I'll check it out tomorrow afternoon. We'll be searching the property."

"Oh, you'll find them. And the legal pad is in her briefcase on the desk in her bedroom—and the note about the Jungle Room is on the counter in the bathroom next to a basket full of makeup. Any word on what they used to poison her?"

The nebulous *they* would be *me* at the moment. As far as the sheriff's department is concerned, I'm still the number one suspect.

Noah glances past me a second before leaning in. "Toxicology is pointing to a homemade remedy. Maybe wolf's bane."

"Wolf's bane?"

"Also known as the devil's helmet, the queen of poison. It's a plant that's easily absorbed into the system, and given the right amount, causes death in minutes. The strange thing is that they didn't find a trace of it anywhere on the table that night. Not in her food, not in yours. They found it in her coffee." I shrink a little because I just so happened to have provided those pumpkin spice lattes. He touches his forehead to mine a moment. "Which brings me to the bit of good news I was coming to give you. Fairbanks and I have officially absolved you as a suspect. There simply isn't enough motive or leads to pursue you any further. And please don't go off and give us any. I mean it, Lottie. You need to step back and let the professionals handle it from here."

"Detective Fairbanks and you." I give a vigorous nod. "You better believe I will. Now that I'm no longer a suspect, I'll be eligible to participate in the pumpkin pie bake-off later this month, and I might even drive home the grand prize—a brand new refrigerated cargo van that will work perfectly for catering events."

"I'm sure you'll take home the grand prize." Noah leans in and lands a lingering kiss to my lips that heats me from the inside out until I reach my boiling point in the very best way.

I pull back and bat my lashes up at him dreamily. "I think I've already won the grand prize." I give his tie a gentle tug, pulling him down to me another notch.

"The winner would be me." He presses his lips to mine a moment. "How about dinner sometime this week? I miss seeing your smiling face."

"Don't give me anything to frown about and you got a deal. I'm open every night. Just give me a holler."

"Will do and don't forget, no funny business. There is a very dangerous person out there who was brazen enough to kill in a room full of people."

"Aye aye, sir." I offer a mock salute. "Say, now that I'm not at the top of the suspect list, who's next on your professional radar?" I'm only half-teasing. Everyone in that room had a beef with Collette.

Noah shakes his head subtly. His expression grows serious as if it were dire news.

"It can't be that bad," I tease. "I hardly knew anyone in that room, so I doubt I'll take it as hard as you are."

"You know him well enough."

"Him?" Mr. Rutherford comes to mind, then Josh the

mouth-to-mouth guy who wasn't to touch her—and then another far more handsome and respectable man pops to mind. "No!" I bark so loud half the park freezes solid for a second.

"Yes. I let him know this morning. He's not too thrilled."

"Will it affect his career? I mean, do they allow judges who are suspects in active homicide investigations to preside over a courtroom?"

"Not for long. He's got five days to clear his name before he's suspended."

"Five days." My goodness, Everett could lose his entire career over this nightmare.

"And that's more than enough time for me to prove he didn't do it." He tips his head to meet my wandering gaze. "*Me* being the operative word. Do we agree on that?"

I hold my tongue a moment because there is not one single part of me that wants to agree. Instead, I nod in lieu of words.

I'm nodding because Noah is gorgeous, and right, and my brand new boyfriend whom I don't want to ruin things with.

"Good." Noah crashes a kiss to my lips, and I don't bother withholding my tongue from him another moment. Noah and I exchange a heart-stopping lip-lock right there under that old faithful oak, in the middle of the day, right here in Honey Hollow.

Noah and I are finally at peace together.

But a small part of me can never really be at peace knowing that Everett only has days before he's forced off the bench.

And I'll do everything I can to make sure that doesn't happen.

CHAPTER 7

*ll night I toss and turn trying to think of ways to help Everett without actually seeing Everett, because to be honest that whole quasi-invisible father figure freaks me out a bit, but I've got nothing.

I get to the Cutie Pie early and bake my heart out, and the bakery is packed with bodies until well past noon. That's when one of my customers informs me she was at the awards banquet last Saturday night and just had to come in for some more of those addicting sweet treats. She casually mentioned that the entire PR firm has been raving about them ever since. Odd, considering the fact one of their own bit the big one while imbibing on a latte that I provided. But what they may not realize is that the sweet treats and the lovely lattes were all born from the same kitchen. As soon as she left, I was hit with a humdinger of an idea and convinced Keelie to help me pull it off.

"You sure we're not going to get arrested?" Keelie's usual bubbling demeanor has been replaced with a morbid dread of the county jail. Both our arms are brimming with giant platters of cookies, and if the wind picks up again, it might just rain pumpkin pinwheels.

"I'm positive," I say, looking into the darkened windows of the Weitez and Winnow, Endeavor PR firm. It's a six-story building made entirely of steel and black glossy windows. There's an air of superiority to the building itself, and I'm willing to bet it's a contagion that's spread to the minions who dwell inside. "Besides, we're simply bringing them a couple of samplers to enjoy as a sign of our appreciation for allowing us to cater that night." A couple of men in business suits exit, looking intimidating with their dark sunglasses—and with no sun in sight—their briefcases heavy with presumably important things. I look to Keelie. "Whatever you do, don't mention Collette Jenner."

We stride in and are greeted with a spacious floor

plan, clean and bright, all steel and Carrera marble. The staircase to our left is made of a series of hard angles, and the railing looks as if it's made of steel string.

A warm face glances up from the front desk, and I press out a smile as we head on over.

"I remember you!" I say a touch too cheerfully to the dirty blonde with a bit of a mischievous look in her eyes. "Collette Jenner introduced you as her best friend."

Keelie steps on my toes so hard the air gets knocked out of my lungs just as efficiently as if she socked me in the gut.

"Oh"—her face crumbles a moment—"that's right. You're the girl who baked the cookies." She points to the trays. "I'm Jenna Hatfield."

"Hi, Jenna. We brought these for the company, for anyone who might want them. I just thought it might be a kind gesture during these trying times."

"By all means, put them down. They'll be gone in ten minutes and mostly by me." She giggles as I peel the plastic wrap off them, and the sweet scents of sugar and vanilla fill the air. She snaps up a brownie dusted in confectioners' sugar and moans into its fudgy goodness. "You really are good at what you do."

"Right." I glance to Keelie and shrug. "And, um, Collette was really good at what she did. I hear the funeral is Saturday. I'm sure we'll be getting the final details soon."

"Oh, I already have them," she says with a mouthful before pulling up her phone. "Noon at the Honey Hollow Covenant Church. Mr. Rutherford and Collette were really close." She averts her eyes when she says it, and it sounds an alarm in me.

"Oh? That's great. I'm really close with my boss, too. In fact, I think of her as a grandmother. I bet Collette felt the same warm paternal feelings." All that kinky garb she has in her dresser drawer leads me to believe otherwise.

A gurgling laugh emits from the girl, and there goes that eye roll again. "Collette didn't think of him as any sort of father figure. Nope, more like a sugar daddy, if you know what I mean." She gives a little wink as she pops a pumpkin spice cookie into her mouth.

Keelie knocks her knee into mine. "Oh, honey, I know all about that. I once dated a higher-up in my company, and his wife was none the wiser. That man had more money and time to burn than I could spend. But we all know what he was really after." A husky laugh pumps from her.

My mouth falls open, unsure of where to take this crazy train next.

Jenna lifts a finger. "Funny you should say that—but let's be honest, that's all he wanted from Collette."

What? Score! I'll have to remember to high-five

Keelie in the car—and not with my fist like I threatened to do if she got out of line.

A deadly thought comes to me. "But wives don't look too fondly on that kind of thing once something of that nature is revealed. In fact, it could make them stark raving mad."

Jenna snatches a honey bar off the tray and waves me off. "Patty couldn't care less who her husband is banging these days." She does a quick sweep of the vicinity before standing up and leaning in. "He's into things that Patricia Rutherford would rather die than do. I should know. He was into them with me, too." She guffaws at the thought, and I elbow Keelie in the ribs until we're cackling right along with her.

"Yeah, some people just don't get it," I say, completely unaware of where I'm going next. "But I get it. And Collette certainly got it."

Keelie nods. "She's the one who really shed a light on things for me. In fact, I credit Collette with where I am right now in my life."

Brill! I bite down on a smile at Keelie's *punny* punch line.

"You, too?" Jenna looks gob-smacked. "It's a lifestyle choice really."

I give an audible gulp. Anytime somebody invokes that term it sends up an internal red flag.

"I agree," I say, hoping she'll take the bait. "What's

that place she told us about?" I snap my fingers at Keelie. "The Romper Room?"

"Ha!" Jenna squawks. "The Jungle Room," she practically mouths the words.

"That's right!" Holy mother of all things good and evil! "It's down in Leeds, right?"

"Yes," she nods enthusiastically.

I shoot Keelie a knowing look. All the down and dirty roads lead to Leeds. Hey? That's catchy! They should look into that as a slogan.

Keelie winces my way. "Told you it was. It's at that nightclub, the girly one. Red Lace?"

"Red Satin," Jenna and I say in unison, and I'm secretly mortified I have so much knowledge in all things down and dirty.

Jenna and I share a laugh and exchange congratulatory high fives.

"I haven't been down that way in months." She dabs the corners of her eyes with her pinkies. "I used to be Collette's side girl, but she got greedy and wanted Rutherford all to herself."

Side girl? I glance to Keelie, and she shrugs.

I clear my throat. "I know all about that greedy side of her. I wanted to be her side girl with Everett, her special friend I'm sure you met that night, but she wasn't having any of it either."

"Ooh!" Her eyes widen with glee. "That cute hunk of

a man she dragged down to the banquet Saturday night? He's a judge, isn't he? Who would have thought he was into ménage?"

"Men—ahh!" A croaking sound comes from my throat, and Keelie quickly waves a crowd over.

"Free cookies!" she trills, and a stampede nearly knocks us to the floor.

I wave to Jenna as the crowd pushes us toward the door. "Stop by the Cutie Pie Bakery and Cakery any time you need a treat! It's on me!" I say, waving and she waves right back.

"We'll see you on Saturday!"

Keelie and I speed out into the icy air. The rustle of birch trees surrounding the building sounds like a line of tambourines.

We get into my car and burst out into a fit of nervous giggles.

"That was enlightening," I say, holding my hand to my chest in an effort to keep my heart from ejecting itself.

"Boy was it ever! Who knew Collette Jenner was such a freak? And with her boss!"

"And don't forget her best friend. I love you Keel, but Noah is off-limits."

She rattles a laugh my way. "So, does that mean Noah and you are ready to take things to the next level?"

My teeth graze over my bottom lip. "I think so. I

mean, I still haven't had a decent moment alone with him. I suppose that's next. But I feel greedy. Have you seen the man?"

Keelie makes crazy eyes, the way she always does when she wants to drive a point home. "Honey, if that was me, we would have been having this conversation a week after I met him. I'm sure he's more than ready to talk about it. In fact, I bet all that boy does is walk around with a goofy grin while thinking about you."

My phone buzzes, and I pluck it out of my purse. "Ha! It's a text from Noah."

"I'm always right. It's pretty scary."

Just arrived at that location I told you about yesterday. Are you sure about the toys in the night-stand? There's no note in the master bath, and there is no sign of a briefcase.

"I think he's at Collette's house," I say numbly. "He mentioned they were going to do a sweep."

Positive. I have the pictures to prove it, remember? I text and hit *send*.

He messages right back. **Hang onto those. I might need them. It looks like someone might have come in and picked the place clean of a few choice items. Unfortunately, this just made my night a heck of a lot longer. We'll have to do dinner some other night. Sorry.**

"Looks as if Noah and I will have to hold off on that conversation another day."

Keelie wrinkles her nose. "At least he's got a job."

"And what a job it is."

Keelie and I head back to Honey Hollow, and all the way there I think about who might have broken into Collette's home and stolen a few choice items. It wasn't me, and I'm pretty sure it wasn't Bear. I'm betting Mr. Rutherford had a thing or two to hide from the world.

Maybe it's best if I pay him a visit.

Or maybe, just maybe, I should start the next leg of my investigation in the Jungle Room.

CHAPTER 8

A good baker understands that the sharpest weapon in her arsenal is a cookie.

I texted Everett earlier today and managed to wrangle out of him the time his final case would most likely be finished. No sooner do I show up in the court-house parking lot than he comes striding out the back entrance, his signature dark inky suit, his briefcase swinging with each step and—GAH! That poltergeist who always manages to catch me off guard floats alongside him as if he were a missing appendage looking to reattach itself.

"Everett!" I jump out from behind a car and watch as his eyes enlarge the size of golf balls. "I come bearing cookies!" I sing as I trot forward with a cute little pink box chock-full of warm peanut butter crunchies. I happen to know they're his favorite. I'm about three steps away when my foot catches on a crack in the asphalt, and both my cookies and me launch into Everett in a crash and smash maneuver.

"Lemon." He helps stabilize me with his arms, and I look up to see a smile daring to twitch on his lips. "What in the world are you up to?"

"I'm glad you asked." I pull a cookie off my chest. "Hungry?"

RED SATIN GENTLEMEN'S CLUB in downtown Leeds is every bit as seedy as I remember. Inside it's dimly lit, the music is bone-shattering loud—in the event they can't hear it on the space station—the entire place holds the scent of stale fries and beer on tap, and scantily clad women dance lazily on stage while men and women alike hoot and holler for them to take it off. Every time a set ends, the girls make their way down into the audience and offer up personal services with which the dancers earn the big bucks, or at least I hope for their sake. I also visited Girls Unlimited last month in an effort to catch Hunter's killer—and that is how I inadvertently became a connoisseur of strip clubs. Girls Unlimited is the place where Stella, the woman who did in fact kill Hunter, jiggled her girl parts. Of course, she's in custody awaiting sentencing, but from what I've gleaned she's getting the proper psychiatric help she needs. Red Satin, however, is the same establishment that houses Martinelle Finances somewhere in an underground lair that I hope to never see again. Although, I'm guessing we're about to be introduced to a whole new wing.

Everett takes in an enormous breath as he gives a look around. "This has quickly become routine for us, Lemon."

"And as I said in the car, this will be the very last time this place sees the likes of me—and hopefully you." Crosses fingers and toes.

A waitress walks by with an empty tray and a look of general despondency. She's wearing nothing but a set of pink sparkling pasties, a matching bowtie, and a thong, and I jump in her way with a friendly wave. It's so loud in here you'd think it was their responsibility to provide the boom box music to every gentlemen's club in Leeds —and Lord knows they have more than their fair share.

And the scent of the fries on her platter is making my stomach growl something awful.

"We're looking for the Jungle Room," I mouth those last two words in the event it's a secret club, with a secret handshake, that you might actually not qualify to be in if you speak its moniker out loud.

She sticks her forefinger and her pinky into her mouth and lets out a whistle that pierces right through the music. A bouncer in a muscle tee that looks about three sizes too small and ears that look as if they've been pinched and turned by a giant nods our way.

"That's our ride," I hiss at Everett. "Do you think you can take him on if things go wrong?"

"Things have already gone wrong, Lemon. Very, very wrong."

We follow Mr. Muscles down a long, dark hall and are led into a dimly lit room where slower, moodier music blares through the speakers. I filled Everett in on everything on the way over, and he only agreed to go along with my little walk on the wild side in exchange for me helping him shake his father's ghost.

Of course, I said yes. Of course, I have no power to make that happen. But Everett doesn't need to know that just yet.

I'm sure Noah would be impressed to see how far I'd go to help a friend keep their career intact. Either that or he'd hightail it right back to Cincinnati. I'm guessing it'd be the latter.

Finally, we're introduced to a woman named *Pink* with eyelashes as long as my arm and a fun, flirty cocktail dress that happens to be missing the entire UPPER TORSO! Her hair is short and frizzy, and her white lips glow like the sun against the black light overhead.

"Singles, couple, or ménage?" she asks just as nonchalantly as if she were taking our order for a burger and fries.

"Couple," I say, pulling Everett in hard. My adrenaline has spiked to unsafe levels, and my body can't stop shaking like a dog at the vet.

The truth is, I feel the very real need to hide behind Everett's body. Every time the volume dips in the music, I hear an errant moan and groan, and it sounds like an outright torture chamber we've wandered into. Leave it to Collette to get one final parting shot at me—by way of whips and chains.

The neon lipped, partial cocktail dress wearing young woman tips her head thoughtfully as she looks past us. "I've got the Aquatic Room available. Of course, the Cave, the Boardroom, or the House of Horrors is open as well. Which one you feelin'?"

Boardroom? House of Horrors? I gag as I look to Everett for help. How are we supposed to glean anything about Collette and her kinky ways if we're locked up in some ridiculous room together? And I have absolutely zero clue what we would do in there.

Everett's lids hood over, and a hint of a naughty grin blooms on his lips as if he knew exactly what we could fill our time with. "Lemon?"

"Down, boy," I growl before turning back to our new friend, Pink. "You know, my friend, Collette Jenner, she came here all the time and she—"

"You knew Coco?" She waves me off as if we were suddenly on another level together. "She and Ruthy loved the Passion Room." She cranes her neck just past us. "It's taken tonight. How's her side girl doing? I heard all about what went down at that awards ceremony. Poor girl should have seen that coming."

Ruthy? That must be Mr. Rutherford. My fingers touch over my lips, and Everett bumps his shoulder to mine as if to say *knock it off*.

"She sure should have," he says while looking at me. "I've been saying the same thing all week."

Pink nods, and it feels as if she and Everett just went to another level without me. "You don't get to be queen without making a few enemies. Once you start throwing parties, everybody thinks they can come. People don't respect the invite. Like that kid that kept coming around." She hooks her finger to her upper lip and studies the floor. "He kept trying to get in on the action, and Coco held firm. She had her hard limits, and he was one of them."

That kid? My mind does a quick scan of the party, and before I can process it, I blurt out, "Josh!"

The whites of her eyes enlarge. "Yeah, that's it! He was a no-fly zone for Cokes. We had security escort him out a few times. I tried to get him into a free-for-all." She hitches her thumb to some nebulous place behind her where all the moaning seems to be coming from and now we know why. A free-for-all with strangers sounds like a perfectly good way to pick up thirteen different communicable diseases, most of which I'm sure they have no cure for.

"Security, huh?" I look to Everett, stunned to hear it. "I bet Coco had an entire fleet of regulars, though. I mean, she didn't have any room to take on someone else." And exactly what in the heck was she doing with these people? *Eww* and *yuck*! On second thought, I don't want to know.

"She had a small handful. Ruthy and Jen were her go-tos. But I'd surprise her on occasion with a few hand-picks I selected myself, and I never disappointed my girl and her crew."

"So, you guys know your way around this stuff or do you need an introduction?"

Everett grunts. "We got this," he says it so fast I almost believe him.

"Well, let's get you going. We're not gettin' any younger." She flicks a finger in the air for us to follow her, and she leads us past several closed doors until she lets us into a room marked *House of Horrors*. I'm sensing a life theme here. "Go on and get your groove on. There's a two-way behind you if you want to open it up. Some people like to be watched. I'll be out front if you need me. Any friend of Coco's is a friend of mine."

The room glows an ethereal shade of blue. Chains and shackles dangle from the ceiling and walls, and there's a box of what looks like discards of Halloween costumes. A bevy of cheap wigs and horrifying masks that I will most likely see in my nightmares for years to come spill onto the floor. There's a rope neatly coiled at our feet like a snake, and to the right there's some sort of rusted gym equipment that I'm not entirely sure how to utilize.

Pink seals the door behind her, and I balk at Everett. "That wasn't hard at all. She practically handfed me all the information I needed," I squeal. "So, what should we do now?"

His lids hang heavy, and his lips curve toward the ceiling. Everett reaches up and flicks a handcuff, making it sway like a pendulum.

"I'd keep it G-rated if I were you. Your father is in the room." I nod to the glowing specter who looks as if he's exceptionally ticked off to be here. "Judging by the venom he's spewing—his entire person is a poison-green color, in the event you were wondering—I'm guessing this kind of a venue wasn't his thing."

"Whoa." Everett lifts his hands as if it were a stickup. "I forgot about that. Do you think he can hear me?"

The specter nods over at his son.

"He says yes."

"Good." Everett turns to look in the direction I just glanced in. "Can you hear me, Father? I don't want you here." His voice riots to deafening decibels. "I didn't need you when you were living, and I sure as hell don't need you now. Get it? Get out of my life. You didn't want to be a part of it when you had a chance, so I don't see why I should give you the privilege now!" His voice booms off the ceiling, and before I can look to see what his father might have to say about it, the door bursts open and in strides Mr. Muscles.

"Everything okay in here?" He jabs a finger my way as if all that shouting was my fault. It sort of was in a roundabout way, but he doesn't have to know that.

"Just fine!" My voice pitches as I jump to Everett's side. "We're just as happy as can be. We were just getting to the good stuff, too." I do my best to shoo him away.

Mr. Muscles folds those tree trunks he calls arms over his enormous chest and casts a suspicious glance my way. "You look familiar. Do I know you?"

"No! No, not at all. I just have one of those faces.

Everyone thinks they went to high school with me. Honey Hollow High! Are you a graduate?"

He shakes his head and shuts the door.

My hand clutches to my chest. "My word, I thought he was going to eat us alive. He thought we were *fakes*! And worse yet, he remembers me! I bet he saw us that day we crashed into Martinelle Finance."

Everett smirks. "Or maybe he spotted you the night you dragged your friends into the club to enjoy the show."

I scoff at the thought. "For your information, Everett, I was not enjoying the show. I was—"

The door swings open once again, and my panic hits an all-time high. The last thing I want is to meet my demise by way of Mr. Muscles, so I do the first thing that comes to mind. I hop up, wrap my legs around Everett's waist, and crash my mouth to his in hopes he'll leave us the heck alone so we can skedaddle like God and Everett's father intended.

Everett presses in close, not fighting my efforts at all, and his lips feel soft against my own. His hard chest feels like I'm perched against a rock.

"*Lottie?*" a frighteningly familiar voice booms, and I jump off Everett and manage to hit my head on a chain dangling from the ceiling, setting them all swinging into one anther like wind chimes.

A man stands at the door in a suit and a svelte gold

tie that gleams in this unnatural light, and it takes a minute for me to see it's—

"Noah?" I stride forward and find Ivy behind him in a tight red dress, her hair slicked back into a bun as if she were about to do a boardroom takedown. "Looking for directions?" I growl over at her.

Her crimson lips spread with a malevolent grin. "None needed. We just left the Passion Room."

I gasp at Noah. "We are leaving this place right now, mister. You're coming with me."

He glares at Everett a moment before taking me by the hand. "You're coming with me."

CHAPTER 9

*oah and I drive all the way back to Honey Hollow in abject silence, cloaked in anger and perhaps a little petty jealousy thrown in for good measure. Just before he pulls into his own driveway, we look over at Everett's and note he's already beaten us home.

I guess that means Ivy drove herself to Leeds. I'm not sure why, but that makes me feel at least a little bit better.

Noah sags into his next breath as he looks to me. "You want to come in?"

"Do you want me to come in?"

"Yes." His head inches back a notch. "I would love for you to come in."

We get out and head on up his expansive wooden porch. Noah's rental looks and feels like a rustic log cabin, not at all an unusual design for this area of Vermont.

He opens the door for me and motions for me to enter first like a true gentleman, and I do so, noting the fact his cologne permeates the place like a warm evening salve. Instantly, I feel better, safer, far less frazzled than I was back in Leeds, that's for sure. The lights flick on, and I'm treated to a cozy cabin interior with exposed wooden walls comprised of whole logs, blond floors to match. There is a pair of matching gray sofas that sit obediently in front of a fireplace with a television hung up above it that's at least twice the size of my own, and there's a small dining room table next to a kitchen that looks modernized with stainless steel appliances and dark stone counters.

"Nice place," I say, taking a step toward the kitchen.

"Are you hungry?"

"Do you cook?" I'm almost amused by the idea.

Noah lands his arms around me and tries his best to frown, but the smile wins out. That dark hair of his offsets those glowing green eyes, and it's safe to say Noah has already taken me in more ways than one.

"Yes, I cook. But only when I happen to remember to go to the grocery store." His dimples press in, and I melt at the sight. "So that option is unfortunately off the table for now. But I can order a mean pizza. I hear Mangia delivers in thirty minutes or less."

"Sounds perfect. I'm starved."

He chuckles as his thumb dances across his screen. "You must have worked up quite an appetite tonight. What would you like on your pizza?"

"Whatever you deem acceptable."

He puts the call in for a large pepperoni with extra cheese and shrugs my way as if asking if that was acceptable, and I give a thumbs-up. Noah switches his phone off when he's done and holds up the black screen for me to see before he lands it on the counter.

"No interruptions," he whispers as his warm breath caresses my cheek.

"No interruptions. I like that." I can't help but note our hips are moving. "Are we dancing?" I wrinkle my nose up at him, my body still moving in time with his.

"I suppose we are. It's a funny thing because I don't dance. I guess this proves you can make me do anything."

"*Anything?*" I cock my head as we share a dull laugh. "So, did you do anything in the Jungle Room with Ivy?"

My affect turns to stone on a dime, and if he so much as hints at something down and dirty with Fairbanks, I'm blowing past him and never looking back. Although, I'm guessing he'd like an explanation himself.

"Yes." His lids hood as he tucks his hand in the small of my back. "We ran an undercover operation, which you and my former stepbrother could have blown sky high."

There's a hint of something just this side of anger in that heated stare of his, and it's only setting my thighs on fire all that much more. "And I happened to hold another undercover operation at the Endeavor offices the other day, and do you know what I saw when I got there? Your cookies. Imagine that."

I suck in a sharp breath and do my best to disappear, but seeing that I'm alive and well, I don't go anywhere.

"Did you happen to find anything out during either of those outings?"

"Lottie." He tips his head back an inch. "You know I can't disclose any details to you. I'm under contract. I took an oath."

"An oath, huh? Fine. I'll let you off the hook. You don't need to say anything. Just blink once if you gleaned nothing and twice if you did." I give his ribs a swift pinch, and he bucks into me, his eyes closing slowly and opening. "Dead end?"

He gives a somber nod. "And you?"

"Why do I get the feeling I'm being pumped for delicate information, Detective Fox?"

"Because you, Lottie Lemon, baker by trade, just so happen to make a darn good investigator."

"I suppose that's true, considering the only reason you were in that facility to begin with was the note I took a picture of that night. So, her place was really picked clean?"

"Just of the stuff you mentioned. If anything else were missing, we wouldn't know it. No obvious disturbances. Nothing rifled or ransacked to our knowledge. No fun stuff in her nightstand." His brows rise as if he were amused.

"Fun stuff, huh? I bet a place like the Jungle Room was a walk in the park for someone like you."

"That's not what I meant. Someone beat us to the punch. And that's exactly why I want you staying away from anything to do with Collette Jenner's investigation." He sighs heavily, and his chest expands and deflates, taking me for the ride along with it. "But I'm not going to stop you, am I?"

I'm slow to shake my head. "Everett might lose his entire career over this mess, and I was with him at the awards ceremony. I know he didn't do this."

His brows dip as if he didn't like what he heard. "Why was he yelling at you tonight?"

My mouth opens, then closes. There simply isn't a

good way to say he was yelling at his dead father's ghost. "It was hard to hear in there."

He shakes his head. "Why are you covering for him?"

"I'm not covering. Besides, we weren't really going to do anything, so we needed something to pass the time. What's better than a shouting match between friends? We couldn't just leave the second they closed the door."

"I caught you with your legs wrapped around his body and your mouth pressed to his." A wry smile pulls at his lips, but that green monster is alive and well, buried in each of his eyes.

"No, actually, you caught me—okay, fine, you caught me. But, in my defense, that bouncer was about to feed us to the mobster lions who run that place. I had to convince him that we meant business or else. There was nothing going on, I promise."

"Mobster lions." He glances to the ceiling. "Oddly that makes sense."

"So, you believe me when I say that there is nothing at all going on between Everett and me?"

Noah takes a breath and pauses as if he were swallowing down his words. "Other than a rather aggressive looking kiss? Not a thing."

I shrink a little in his arms. "You know there is nobody else out there for me but you. Not even Everett. I love you, Noah."

"And I love you, Lottie Lemon." His lids hood to slits.

"So, tell me, who's the better kisser?"

"I don't know..." It takes everything in me to resist the urge to giggle. "I might need a refresher." My finger outlines his lips, and he opens his mouth and pretends to take a bite out of it.

"Hey, you scared me." I can't help but bubble with a warm laugh, our hips still moving in time.

"You scared me, Lottie Lemon. And you do scare me. Please, if you have any regard for my sanity, let tonight be the last of it. No more injecting yourself in this investigation."

"That sounds like a threat, Detective Fox." My mouth inches toward his.

"That wasn't a threat. This is." Noah crashes his lips over mine, and his tongue swims its way into my mouth as we indulge in a kiss far more daring than we ever have before. His chest presses hard over mine, and he pulls me in by the back of the neck, his fingers digging into my hair, weaving circles through it. My hands ride over his chest as my fingers spread wide and fan over his steely girth. Noah Fox is all man, one hundred percent walking, talking testosterone with just enough of a dangerous side to hold my attention for a long, long time. His kisses increase in ferocity, as do mine, and before I know it, I'm against the wall, his hands riding lower over my hips, his mouth on the nape of my neck.

An abrupt knock erupts over the door and we freeze

solid, the two us glancing in the direction of a hostile deliveryman.

"Should I get that?" He runs kisses up to my ear.

"Only if you don't want the sheriff's department knocking down your door at some point this evening. With the whole town on edge, a simple dismissal of a large pep might be enough to send the SWAT team into action."

"Good point." Noah pays the guy, and soon enough we're snuggled on his sofa while an old rerun plays on TV.

"This pizza is amazing." I moan through my next bite.

"You're amazing." He touches his foot to mine.

"Yeah? Why's that?" I tease, indulging in one last bite before landing my plate back on the coffee table.

"Because you're tenacious and you'd do anything, including risking life and limb, for those you care about." He lands his plate back on the table as well. I think we must have had four slices apiece. "So tell me—" He pulls me over and wraps his arms around me as we watch the crackle of the fire, and suddenly I feel as if I'm in some romantic movie. "What, if anything, did you glean tonight? We're on the same team, remember?" He runs a line down my nose and pats my lips with his finger.

"Oh, I see how it goes. When it's me doing all the

work, we're on the same team." I reach up and take a playful bite out of his cheek. "But I suppose you're right and you are the one bound by law not to share anything, not me." I start in on my conversation with Jenna Hatfield, which, of course, led me to the exact location of the Jungle Room and then the strange conversation I had with Pink and the fact it implied Josh was trying to get in on the kinky fun.

"That's it?" He tucks his head back to get a better look at me. Noah's wheels are turning. His eyes look as if they're oscillating, unsure of where to focus at the moment.

"Isn't that enough?" A laugh bubbles from me. "I happen to think that in addition to running a bakery, I accomplished quite a bit this week."

"That you did." He looks past me, his face heavy with concern. "The thing is, we've already investigated Josh Normandy, and he checks out squeaky clean. It turns out, Collette filed a disturbance claim against him at work. But Rutherford—now that's a new angle for sure."

"What about the wife? Apparently, she doesn't mind all the side action. Is that the craziest thing you've ever heard? She doesn't *mind*!"

He winces. "I hate to say it, but I've seen it again and again. His libido doesn't match hers, and soon they're not only in separate bedrooms but he's looking elsewhere to scratch that itch with the wife's blessing."

"We'll never get like that," I purr into him, and no sooner do the words string from my lips than I regret them.

The air stills around us as a slow budding smile graces his lips. Noah smiles with his whole face, his eyes holding their own naughty affect. "No, I don't think we will." His finger glides gently over my cheek.

"I think I'm ready to take that next step with you," I say it low and quiet in the event if he didn't want to hear it he can pretend he didn't. But who are we kidding? Noah is a guy. He's probably working out the logistics of how fast he can get me into his bedroom.

"I think I'm ready, too." That determined look in his eyes sharpens for a moment. "And I think we should wait."

"*Wait?*" I'm mortified. Never in my life have I met a man who wanted to wait, and suddenly my every attribute is called into question.

"Yes." He pecks a quick kiss to my lips. "I want this to be special. You're special to me, Lot. I don't plan on going anywhere. I want to do everything in life with you. I want to build memories with you. I think maybe this is a great place to start."

"Memories?" I sigh. "You do realize I'm swooning. Is this the part when we pick a date? Thanksgiving is just around the corner. What is there better to be thankful for than each other?"

"Thanksgiving is perfect, except for the fact I'm pretty sure you'll be exhausted from baking everyone in Honey Hollow a pie or two to go with their meal."

"You are so right. And I sort of have a bad habit of staying up for three days in a row once Black Friday hits. How about the weekend after? It's the beginning of December right before the big holiday rush? I can try to take the weekend off, and we can have a little getaway at your place and mine."

"Your place and mine." He rumbles with a laugh. "I like that. And I like that you always have a way of keeping me on my toes."

"Get used to it. I don't see me changing anytime soon."

"I will make a note of that."

My finger glides down his chest in the shape of a soft S. "So, what do you propose we do now?"

His lids hood with devilish intent. "Practice a few select moves and pray the next two weeks go by in a flash."

A laugh bucks through me. "I second that."

Noah and I practice well into the night and into the early hours of the morning.

Noah and I are taking our time, making memories, making everything right.

Never before have I felt so deeply loved.

Never before have I been so thoroughly terrified.

CHAPTER 10

⁓

*B*aking for friends and family always adds a layer of passion to the treats I'm making, and since I consider everyone who sets foot in the bakery a friend, I'm always adding love into the mix. And when Jackie Jenner, Collette's poor mother, asked if I would cater the wake, it was an offer I would never refuse.

"Lily, we need to get all of these cookies on platters and delivered to Carlson Hall in two hours. Will you be going to the funeral?" Thanks to Keelie, the Cutie Pie Bakery and Cakery is almost at capacity with a staff of its own, so if Lily wanted to go, she certainly could. I imagine she was closer to Collette than I was.

Lily tosses that long, dark mane of hers. I've never seen hair with more body than that on Lily. She's always been one of the prettier girls in Honey Hollow, but one of the meanest to go along with it, and for that reason alone I've never let any part of her intimidate me.

"Will that hot judge be there?" Her eyes flash with wicked intent before she gets back to arranging the platters.

"Everett? Yes, of course. He and Collette dated for a while." Good Lord in heaven knows I want zero details about what they might have done during their tumultuous tenure together.

"Then I'm in." She quickly unties her apron and heads for the back.

"Where are you going?" I call after her.

"If that judge is there, I need to get ready. You said yourself we've only got two hours!"

"Will you be back to help deliver these platters?"

"As soon as I get my stilettos on." She gives a suggestive lift of the shoulder before heading out into the chilled autumn air.

The rest of the staff steps in, and I get busy putting the last of the cookies onto the cooling racks. Jackie gave a list of all of Collette's favorite goodies, and I've baked them all in number—hazelnut crinkle cookies, jumbo coconut chocolate chip, caramel drizzled almond bars, pecan tassies, cinnamon buttercups, apple walnut bars, brownies and blondies, peanut butter squares topped with fudge, toffee crisps, chocolate tipped short-bread, and, of course, pumpkin pinwheels. I thought of bringing along a few pumpkin pies, seeing that we're so close to Thanksgiving, but I didn't want anyone to associate the treat with such a sad occasion—sales for my pumpkin spice lattes have plummeted after it was disclosed it was poisoned with wolf's bane. Besides, I still need to get full clearance with the contest council in Ashford so I can participate in the upcoming bake-off. They had asked for an official letter from the sheriff's department, and Noah hand-delivered it to the head of the council a few days ago. The bakery really needs that van, and I just know my pumpkin pie is as good as and perhaps better than the rest. So I definitely have a shot at winning. I hope.

A couple of women step into the bakery, and I head to the front and take their orders.

"Coffee and two slices of pecan pie," the older of the two commands. She looks right up there with Nell, late eighties, early nineties maybe, and she shakes her head as if she were angry about something.

And the younger woman dressed in a dark shawl

with a beaded necklace that glitters under the twinkle lights above nods in agreement.

I hand them their orders on adorable miniature silver platters. My mother found a handful at an estate sale and thought it would be a cute way to serve my customers who wanted to stay in the café to enjoy their treats.

"Everything all right, ladies?" I'm betting they're headed to the funeral. They both look far too formally dressed for a Saturday.

The Nell lookalike waves me off. "We just can't get over the rash of gruesome murders and break-ins that have hit Honey Hollow. This used to be a safe place, and now you practically need to head to the city to flee the violence." They share a quiet chortle at the thought.

"But the garage robberies have stopped, so that's a good thing, right?" I know for a fact they stopped because it was poor Hunter who was doing them, and he's no longer with us.

"I don't know." The woman in the dark shawl takes a sip from her coffee. "I live across the street from our dearly departed Collette, and I saw someone entering her house the very night she was murdered. Imagine that. Why, that woman had the worst luck of anyone I knew."

I shrink a little behind the counter because I'm pretty sure the woman she saw was me. A thought occurs to me. Maybe she didn't see me? Maybe she saw the real thief? And I bet he or she was the killer!

"Oh, I heard about that." I shake my head, dismayed —literally by my own actions. "Did they catch the thief? I mean, does anyone even know what they look like?" Gah! They? Way to implicate yourself. Why don't I just show her the pictures I took while I'm at it?

"It wasn't a they." She's quick to admonish. "It was most certainly a *she*. A blonde woman ran into the house. I saw it myself. Of course, at that hour I didn't realize what had happened to poor Collette, so I didn't think much about it. She was a busy person and had a busy social life to boot. There were always men and women running in and out of there at all hours." She shrugs as if she were indifferent to it.

I think on this for a moment. My hair is often mistaken for blonde, and if that streetlamp, which happened to be seizing that night, shone over me, I would certainly look so.

"So, you saw that truck?" I shake my head, hoping she didn't. "I mean, I heard whispers of it myself."

"That's the thing." She lifts a crooked finger. Her bright orange lipstick is drawn in a line over her mouth. "I don't know what the other neighbors think they saw, but there wasn't a truck. It was a red sedan. Cherry red, I tell you. And she came out with a bag. I saw it with my own two eyes."

A bag!

"Have you told the police?"

"No, I don't want any trouble. If this madman who's been running around slaughtering our own townspeople isn't caught soon, I'll have my house for sale come spring." They scuttle off to the nearest table, still grumbling into their coffee.

Red sedan. Cherry red.

I think I'll head to the funeral a little early and hang out in the parking lot in the event that blonde decides she'd like to pay her respects.

OF EVERY MODE of transportation that showed up before the funeral began, there wasn't a cherry red sedan in the bunch. Figures.

Everett asked if I would sit with him, and, of course, I'm more than happy to oblige. It's Everett on one side of me and his deceased father on the other. A little unnerving, considering the fact he's no longer in the material. The funeral is full of showy wreaths and even showier people. I've never seen so many designer labels in a room at once. And don't get me started on the perfume and cologne thick as fog. It's like being stuck at ground zero in the perfume aisle at the mall. There's no casket, just an oversized picture of Collette, all smiles, looking her best. It's black and white, which is a shame because she really did have such pretty red hair.

Mr. Rutherford and his wife, Patricia, are seated near the front. Mr. Rutherford looks as if he's holding strong, and Mrs. Rutherford looks bored as if she'd rather be anywhere but the funeral of her husband's mistress. I crane my neck and spot Josh Normandy, the kid who tried to burst into Collette's wild party at the Jungle Room and who did finally get a piece of the action when he gave her mouth-to-mouth. A lot of good that did. Unlike the Rutherfords, he indeed looks pretty broken up about Collette. There's a wad of tissues in his hand, and his eyes are beet red and swollen. He seems to be hanging onto every word the minister is saying.

Soon enough, her mother, Jackie, takes the pulpit and says a few kind words about her daughter, as does Collette's brother, Steven. Once he takes his seat, there's a long spate of silence, and just as the minister is about to take the helm once again, the back door bursts open and in runs Jenna Hatfield with a bright red coat and a pink scarf around her neck.

"I'm here!" she cries out as she dashes to the front. "Oh gosh, I'm here, and I'm late to my best friend's funeral!" A light chuckle bounces through the room.

The minister waves her up, and she takes off her coat, revealing a shocking pink dress before scooting her way to the pulpit. Her cheeks are flushed, her hair wild and frizzy.

"I'm so sorry I'm late. The battery in my car died, so I had to beg my neighbor to give me a jump. Of course, there was roadwork on the way over, and by the time I got to Honey Hollow, all of the streetlights malfunctioned. Just my luck." She guffaws into the microphone, and the sound of her stale laughter reverberates off the walls.

She looks to Collette's oversized picture, that eerie grimace frozen in time. It's almost not fair. Nobody told Collette that very snapshot would one day represent her at her own funeral. It's a terrible thing really. Because if she knew, I guarantee she wouldn't be smiling so hard. But I suppose that's the best way to remember her.

"Dear Collette"—she tries her best to control her panting—"I suppose it's fair to say you had a charmed life overall, but nobody had worse luck than you on that fated night."

A series of gasps circles the room.

"I'm sorry!" Jenna holds a hand out. "I had a speech prepared. I suppose I should stick to the script or who knows what might come flying out of this mouth." She pats herself down before plucking a folded note from her bra, and another round of chuckles ensues. "Ah, yes. Here we go. My dearest Collette, here I am at the one place I never wanted to be and neither did you." She pauses to offer a soft smile up at the crowd before holding the paper at arm's length. "That's better. So, as you can see, I've obeyed your wishes and did not wear black to your funeral. I am not sad. And I did my best not to cry too much. Our friendship is one to be rivaled through the ages. You were my rock when things got tough, and I would like to think I was the same for you. There isn't anything I wouldn't do for you. In fact, I've already done what a good best friend would do. There is nothing for you to worry about. No embarrassment, no humiliation, no reason to fear. All you need to do now is rest well, my dear." She giggles into the mic. "I guess that last part rhymed, didn't it?" She looks over at Jackie and nods. "I'm sorry. She was a special woman and will be very much missed."

No sooner does she take a seat than the church goes dark and a brief video montage plays. Collette looks expressive and vibrant in each and every photo, and it really is heartbreaking that she was taken away from this world so soon. Suddenly, I feel charged to find the killer, not just for Everett, but for Collette as well.

I glance back toward Jenna and think about my own blonde bestie. Surely, if something untimely happened to me, she would do what any best friend would do as well. There would certainly not be anything to fear or to be embarrassed—OH MY WORD!

I glance to Everett and smack him on the arm.

He tips his head up at me as the lights come back on and bodies begin to drain next door to Carlson Hall for refreshments.

Everett wraps his arm around my shoulders as he leans in close. "What's going on?"

"I think I just discovered who broke into Collette's home that night after I did."

His brows pinch hard in the middle. "You broke into Collette's home?" he hisses just above a whisper.

I give a quick glance around. "Only to look around and I found some kinky goodies, too. *Sex* toys—plus, that's initially where I learned about the Jungle Room. But when Noah and Ivy went to look around, those things were gone. I spoke with someone at the bakery today, and she confirmed there was a blonde who showed up later that night in a red sedan and came out with a bag."

"And?"

"I'm willing to bet Jenna Hatfield drives a red sedan."

CHAPTER 11

*E*verett and I—and his ever-present father, file out of the church and hungrily look for a cherry red sedan in the parking lot but to no avail.

"I think I found it," Everett whispers and points across the street at a rather hastily parked cherry red sedan.

"That must be it! You did it! *We* did it!" I lunge over him with a hearty embrace just to find Noah standing behind him flashing a manufactured smile my way.

"What exactly did the two of you do now?" Noah's affect falls flat again, and I'm quick to disembark from Everett.

"Nothing." I hop over and land a chaste kiss to Noah's lips just as Ivy comes up from behind. "Detective Fairbanks," I say without letting go of my man, and she openly scowls at me.

"Lemon." She nods to Everett. "Judge Baxter. I'll be inside with the refreshments. Detective Fox, please mind what we discussed." She takes off for the set of opened doors behind us as a flood of bodies fill the hall.

"Mind what we discussed? Do you *mind* sharing what that might be?"

He glances to Everett. "Only if you mind sharing what put you in such a celebratory mood when I came upon you."

Everett glowers at Noah a moment too long, and if I'm not mistaken, his father does the same. "Lemon, I leave that entirely up to you. I think I'll join Detective Fairbanks inside." He takes off, and Noah wraps his arms around my waist.

"You don't have to tell me. In fact, if it doesn't involve a strip joint or an underground sex club, I'm good with not knowing for now."

A choking sound emits from my throat. "You really don't want to share whatever secret you and Ivy have, do you?"

He grimaces. "It's not necessarily a secret. Let's just say some information is best kept under wraps until it's proven to be true."

"I fully agree with that." I just hate that there are question marks between us. But as much as I crave open and honest, there are some things I just can't bring myself to share with Noah. At least not yet. I rather like the fact he finds me sane—for now. "How about we head in and I take you right to the platter of chocolate chips cookies I snuck over just for you?" It's true. I had an inkling he might show up.

"You do love me."

"That I do."

Inside the hall it's thick with bodies, which in turn brings up the temperature in the room. Intermittent bouts of laughter emit, but mostly it's a somber scene with old friends catching up with one another and upcoming holiday plans being exchanged. I spot Lainey and the forever hair flipper Tanner Redwood talking to a few of Lainey's friends from the library. Tanner is a two-timer. Everyone knows that but my sister. I just hate that she and Forest unraveled like a cheap sweater. And even more than that, I hate that Lainey has kept close to Tanner ever since. At first, it was just to make Forest crazy. Lainey rather liked the idea of him wanting to scratch his eyeballs out with jealousy. But now they've sort of come to an understanding that they're together. I'm not sure if Tanner has fully gotten the memo, considering I've spotted him around town with other girls on a few occasions, but when I presented the information to Lainey, she didn't seem too bothered about it, which made me wonder if they had some sort of agreement. Nonetheless, adjacent to them, speaking to the chief of the fire department, is Forest himself. And he's not paying attention at all to what the chief is saying. His jealous eyes are pinned right on my beautiful sister.

Noah leans in. "Looks like Mr. Rutherford is coming our way."

I jump a little as both he and his wife appear before us and offer pleasant smiles.

"Mr. Rutherford, Mrs. Rutherford." I nod to the two of them. "It's so nice to see you again. I'm sorry it wasn't under better circumstances."

"Yes, well"—he turns to look at the giant picture of Collette now being moved from the church to the front of the hall—"I wanted to thank you personally for delivering those platters of delicious cookies to the office last week. It really did provide the morale boost we needed. Spirits have been down ever since we lost our bright light. And I wanted to thank you for catering the awards ceremony as well. Collette let me know earlier that evening that you were making pumpkin spice everything just for me." He gives a soft chuckle.

"That I did. And I hope before the evening turned disastrous, you had an opportunity to enjoy a little of it." Keelie said that Naomi told her they ended up scrapping every last cookie into the dumpster once the forensics team was through investigating. To think all those hours of baking and no one to enjoy it.

"Oh, I sure did." He nods vigorously. "In fact, the pumpkin spice latte was to die for."

His wife, Patricia, smacks him on the arm. "Please excuse my husband. He has no decorum when it comes to funerals. I'd best get him home before he goes and says all sorts of inappropriate things as he's prone to." She lifts a finger as she speeds him to the door, and I watch as they snuggle into their coats before heading out into the overcast day.

"Noah? What do you think would prompt a woman to stay with a man whom she knows is cheating on her? I can't figure it out for the life of me."

He grunts as he glances to the door. "Security. Fear of being on your own in life. Divorce is messy, costly. It can sure turn your world inside out before you know it."

"I guess so, but I wouldn't nearly be as tolerant."

His chest vibrates with a laugh. "Duly noted." He leans in and presses a soft kiss to my ear. "And I promise that you will never have to worry about it."

Ivy waves him down from deep in the crowd, and he sighs. "Duty calls. I'll be back." He takes off, and I spot

Jenna at the cookie table loading up a dessert plate until it's heaping so I make my move.

I speed over and snatch up a dessert plate of my own and throw on a few pieces of German chocolate cookies.

"You did great today," I say as somber as possible, and she does a double take in my direction.

"It's you! The cookie girl. Yup, I meant every single word. Trust me, I wouldn't be wearing this bubble gum getup for anyone else."

"Well, I'm glad you made it in time. And after all that trouble you had on the road, I think it's a miracle you found a parking spot in the lot."

"Oh, I didn't." She takes a bite out of an almond snowdrift and moans. "I ended up parking across the street."

Winner winner best friend dinner!

I glance over at Everett in the distance and he nods my way, but my work isn't finished here just yet.

"But your eulogy was just beautiful. You really loved her. My best friend and I are pretty close, too. And I completely understood what you meant about doing anything for her." A huff of a laugh bucks through me as I lean in close. "In fact, we have a pact. If anything should happen to either one of us, we're to hightail it over to one another's homes and do a little housekeeping in the bedroom, if you know what I mean."

Jenna belts out a monstrous laugh, and half the room

lulls to a whisper for less than two seconds. She leans in, an impish gleam in her eye.

"We made the same pact."

I gasp with delight. "And did you uphold your end of the bargain?"

"Yup. I sure did. But my goodness, I had almost forgotten. Anyway, it was done in the nick of time. You know, it always sounds good in theory, but it was a tough thing to do knowing she would never head back into that bedroom. But I figured she wouldn't want her mother or, heaven forbid, her brother to find those things we girls like to play with."

Eww. "Yes, I totally agree. You are truly a good friend, Jenna." I look to Everett and frown. Lily Swanson has planted herself staunchly by his side, filling his head with gibberish, I'm sure. But his father stands with arms folded across his see-through chest just staring at me as if he wanted answers. "Hey? You knew Collette best. Who do you think would do something so horrible to her?"

She groans as she looks into the crowd. "Collette had more enemies than she had friends, but I can't imagine anyone actually trying to kill her. I mean, she did tick a lot of people off, though."

"Who did she tick off last? You know, at the office?"

"That's easy. That would be Jules King."

"Jules? I think I met her the night of the ceremony. Dark, straight hair?"

"Looks like a Halloween skeleton." Her chest pulsates with a laugh. "It's just us girls. You can say it. Jules and Collette were both up for the VIP award—and as some might suggest, Jules did land three new corporate clients for the firm this year."

"And how many did Collette bring in?"

"None. She was too busy sleeping with the boss." She waves past me and excuses herself.

Jules King. That's the woman I saw arguing with Collette that night. Huh. I do a quick sweep of the room but come up empty.

Everett pops up—ironically along with his Pops.

"Hey, Everett? If someone stole a position of honor at your courthouse, you wouldn't consider murder, would you?"

"I wouldn't, but that doesn't mean someone else with far more rage would do the same. Why? Did you find the killer?"

"Maybe. But I don't see her here. I still have some investigating to do." I glance to his father and blink a shy smile.

"Well, Lemon, once you set your mind to something, you are determined." He looks to me sternly. "As is my father. I saw you glancing to my side. He's here, isn't he?"

"Rest assured, he's always here." I shrug. "And, believe me, I have no idea why."

Everett threads his arm through mine and flashes that rarely seen smile my way, scant and brief as it may be. "Brace yourself, Lemon. We're about to find out."

CHAPTER 12

*E*verett hustles us right out the door, into the windy afternoon and around to the side of the building where there's a patch of grass and a small fountain. It's secluded and socked in between the church and the hall, so there's a bit of a reprieve from the blustery weather.

"Let's have it, Pops." Everett looks around every which way. I point next to the fountain to orient him.

"What's going on? Were you here to warn us of Collette's passing?"

The older, far more determined version of him offers a solemn nod.

"He says yes." My adrenaline kicks in because I've never actually had anything even close to a conversation with a ghost before.

"Okay." Everett lets this soak in a moment. "Are they going to arrest me? Am I going to be wrongfully sentenced? Sent to the electric chair?"

"Geez, Everett," I hiss as I take a step back. "You're going to be fine. I'm this close to finding out who the killer is. Please do not fill your head with thoughts of the electric chair of all things."

His father offers another solemn nod.

"And he agrees with me." I point hard toward the fountain. "Everett, I get that you're worried, and I don't want you to be."

"I called Noah last night. He let me know it wasn't looking good. Fairbanks had something on me, and he wouldn't say what."

"That must be what he was keeping from me. Everett, I'm so sorry." My heart plummets to middle earth just thinking about how terrifying this must be for him.

"Anyhow, one problem at a time. Ask my father what

he wants. I'm pretty sure he doesn't want to be here any more than I want him here."

"What's his name?"

"Edward." He casts his gaze to the ground. "His name was Edward. He was a judge in Fallbrook for decades. That bench was his wife. It was his family. We hardly saw him. One day he and my mother went at it, and he simply moved out. He was hardly interested in us. In fact, he died doing what he loved. Had a heart attack."

"Edward," I say, looking right at the handsome spook. "You heard your son. Is there any way that you can communicate what it is you're doing here?"

He glowers at the building a moment before gliding his forefinger across his neck and pointing hard at the church.

"He just slit his throat and pointed to the church," I relay to Everett. "So you were here to warn us, me, about Collette's impending doom. Is it because she didn't have pets?" I realize how ridiculous it sounds, but hearing it makes it feel twice as unbelievable.

He offers a hearty nod.

"He says yes," I say. "And what about her relatives? Did you volunteer because you wanted to somehow communicate with your son again?"

His chest expands as if he took a ghostly breath, and he nods slowly as he looks to Everett.

"He said yes, Everett. He's come back for you. I'm guessing the two of you have unfinished business?"

Everett's blue eyes tear up in an instant, and he gives a hard sniff as if to avert any further emotions. "Okay. Let's have it. What unfinished business?"

The older version of him takes a step in close to his son. He shakes his head and touches his throat as if highlighting his inability to express a thing. He lays his hand over Everett's head, and Everett closes his eyes as if he can feel him.

"Is this about the way he left my mother, my sister, and me?"

He nods, and I relay it to Everett.

Everett takes a breath. "He wishes it never happened?"

He nods vigorously, and I relay it again.

"He's here to apologize, make amends." Everett pushes the words out as he comes to a sorrowful conclusion.

The older version of him doesn't nod this time. Instead, he wraps his arms around his son, and a spark of light fills his ghostly body.

Everett returns the gesture, embracing his father as if he was solid, and his chest bucks silently as they hold one another like that for a good long while.

"I forgive you," Everett whispers as his father steps

back and looks at his son with all the love and affection a father can.

"I wish you could see how he's looking at you," I whisper.

"I can." Everett continues to look into his father's glowing eyes, and ever so slowly that older version of him begins to dissipate. He points to himself, then folds his arms across his chest before pointing to Everett. "I love you, too, Pops. I really do."

And just like that, he's gone.

"Lemon." Everett's chest expands as he glances to the sky. "We won't speak of this to anyone."

"Never." I hop over and wrap my arms around him. "You're so very lucky, Everett. You don't know how many people would give anything to have just one more chance, one more moment."

He leans in and sniffs into my hair. "I couldn't have done it without you. I guess it was divine intervention we met that day."

"I guess it was."

A set of footsteps clop over. "Well, look what we have here."

I pull back as if jumping out of a fire, only to find Detective Fairbanks and a wild-eyed Noah.

"Lottie?" Noah looks a little hurt, and my heart squeezes tight in my chest just witnessing it.

Ivy turns to him. "I guess she didn't leave you after

all, Fox. But it looks as if she might be leaving you in a less proverbial way." She looks to the parking lot before hightailing it out of here. I bet that's where she parked her broom.

"I'm not leaving you." I avert my eyes at the thought.

Everett looks to me, then Noah. "Look, it's not what you think. The funeral stirred up emotions about my father that I didn't expect, and Lemon followed me out here. She was simply comforting me in my time of grief." He nods my way. "Thank you for that," he says as he takes off for the lot himself.

"You're a good friend, Lottie." Noah reels me in, and I relax over his chest as if it were my new home. "I just wish you weren't such a good friend to my former brother." He frowns at the fountain behind me. "I'm sorry. It's silly of me to say."

"No, I get it." I hike up on the balls of my feet and brush a kiss over his lips. "If I'm being perfectly honest, I'm not entirely thrilled you have to spend so much time with Ivy—and never mind how insane it makes me that the two of you are keeping secrets."

A dull laugh rumbles through him. "Only because you want the upper edge on the investigation."

I'm about to tell him that I'm pretty certain I have the upper edge but think better of it.

"Never mind that." I pull him in closer by the tie. "Did you find the answers you were looking for?"

"Maybe. But, in truth, I think we only came away with more questions. And you?"

"Um—same." I shrug. There's no way I'm handing Jules King to Ivy on one of my delicious cookie platters. When I'm good and certain, I'll tell Noah and he can make the arrest. And then Keelie's father, the captain of the sheriff's department, will see what an asset he is and take him off probation—and if I'm lucky, he'll fire Ivy for being useless.

Noah tips his head into my line of vision. "You have a naughty look in your eye. Am I going to like what you're thinking?"

"I think you are very much going to like what I'm thinking. I have the bakery staffed for the rest of the day. How about we grab a pizza and cuddle up with Pancake and a movie at my place?"

"You're right. I very much like what you're thinking." His brows bounce, and that crooked grin graces his face. "Well, Detective Fox, I think pizza is my new favorite food group." I give his tie a tug as I touch my nose to his.

"I think I've got a hankering for something a little sweeter."

Noah lands a kiss over me that's far sweeter, far more demanding and exciting than anything I could whip up in the kitchen.

Noah's kisses taste a lot like love.

WE PULL up to Country Cottage Road and are immediately greeted with the strobe of the flashing lights on top of at least a half dozen police cruisers. I look over to where they are and gasp.

"They're at Everett's house."

Noah and I park in haste, facing the wrong way, and we hop out and run over to the two-story home that sits next to mine.

"Everett!" I call out as he stands next to a sheriff's deputy.

He excuses himself and walks our way.

"What hap—" I don't even finish the question before my eyes land on the malfeasance. Scrawled in dripping red paint across his white double door entry is the word *murderer*. The window next to the door has a giant hole in it and shattered glass sparkles over the porch. "I'm so sorry."

"Just kids, probably." He looks indifferently toward the damage. "They tossed a brick inside before they left. No one saw anything. Apparently, the entire neighborhood was at the funeral."

"Any security cameras?" Noah's eyes shoot at the four corners of the house at once.

"Not yet." Everett sighs. "I'm having them installed Tuesday. It looks like I was off by three days."

"I've got 'em." Noah gives my hand a squeeze. "I've got one pointed at Lottie's just in case. I'll go see if it caught anything." He takes off to speak with the deputies, and a couple of them head across the street with Noah.

"You're right. It was probably just kids—*teenagers*," I say it with all the angst I can muster. "Your name is going to be cleared very, very soon."

"Not soon enough. The city council contacted me yesterday and asked me to step down until I'm no longer a suspect."

I suck in a quick breath. "Everett! I don't know what to say." My hands cover my mouth, and I take him in like this, stoic, strong even in the face of adversity.

He pulls back and swallows hard. "It's okay. Although, I will confess, I wish my father would have hung out a little longer. Now that we're no longer locked in a feud, I'd rather prefer he was with me."

"That's very sweet."

"I guess I'll have to opt for the next best thing."

"What's that?"

"A girl by the name of Lily Swanson invited me out to dinner."

"*No!*" My voice resonates a little too much punctuation for someone who's just friends with Everett, and I hate that.

"I did say no. I'm going to dinner with Fiona instead."

"Fiona Dagmeyer?" I'm not feeling so great about her either. Fiona is a defense attorney that works down at the courthouse with him. And she also happens to be one of his infamous exes. She's a gorgeous brunette, smart as a whip, and quite possibly Everett's last hope—that is, unless I come through for him.

"They don't call her The Dagger for nothing. I figure I'd better stay one step ahead of the sheriff and lawyer up as they say."

"I'd hate for you to bear the expense, especially since your name will be cleared in no time." Like as soon as I get my hands on Jules King.

"Don't worry about that. Fiona doesn't charge me. At least not in dollars." He gives a quick wink as he heads toward the sheriffs.

Noah comes back shaking his head. "The camera is too high and square on your house. I'll have to get another one and point it his way."

"Aren't you the knight in shining armor. Hey, Everett just told me the city council asked him to step down while the investigation was underway. Is there any possibility you can clear his name by Monday?"

Noah winces. "I wish I could. Lottie, what I'm about

to tell you is for your ears only. Do not, and I repeat, do not say a word to anyone, least of all Everett."

"I won't say a word, I promise." My heart drums into my throat as if he were about to give me devastating news, and I think he might be.

"We have solid evidence that Everett placed a powder-like substance into Collette's mug that night."

"What?" My entire body tingles with disbelief. There's no way it's possible. I was with Everett for most of the night—with the exception of that big argument he had with Collette. My word, he didn't really have it out for Collette, did he?

"I wouldn't kid about something like that. We have it on tape."

"Did you ask him about it?"

He looks past me at Everett. "We just reviewed the evidence yesterday. It was like looking for a needle in a haystack, but we got the footage off a cell phone of someone who was at the ceremony that night. A few people voluntarily turned in their phones because they had been taking footage of the event. Unfortunately, that's what we stumbled upon."

"He's not guilty, and we both know it."

Noah closes his eyes a moment as he looks over to Everett. "He sure as hell looks it."

A heavy sigh expels from me.

He sure as hell does.

CHAPTER 13

*B*aking requires both common and uncommon ingredients. I've secured some of the more exotic ingredients all the way from Italy, and others can be purchased at the local grocery store. Every ingredient needs to be measured carefully so it can best accomplish its purpose, and I'm betting that's exactly how the killer went about preparing the wolf's bane.

Keelie leans over my shoulder. "What's wolf's bane?"

"Would you *shush?*" I seal my laptop closed and glance at the customers seated around me at the Cutie Pie Bakery and Cakery. The paper turkeys and cornucopias brimming with pumpkins give this place a fun festive feel for the upcoming holidays, and I'd hate to break the spell with talk of poison of all things. "Noah thinks that's what they used to kill Collette," I whisper.

"It sounds deadly."

"It is. According to the information I was able to find, the proper name is Aconitum, and it stems from the sunflower family. You can only grow it in certain climates—and just a little can be deadly. Whoever was able to slip this into her drink knew exactly what they were doing, and they are most likely a gardener or have had access to this plant."

"Maybe we should go to that garden club our mothers belong to?" She slides into the seat across from me, her eyes never leaving mine. "I want to help you catch this killer." I shared with her all about Everett's predicament, and I was about to share some far more intimate things regarding Noah and me, but we were interrupted.

"The Horticulture Hotties? I think if I showed up out of the blue and began asking about poisonous plants, I might raise an eyebrow or two. Discovering three bodies in three months has sort of put a pox on me socially. I'm lucky the bakery hasn't been affected."

"Speaking of *hotties*"—Keelie bubbles with laughter before she can get the words out—"I do believe you were about to tell me all about your special night with a certain detective. Did things get steamy? Is my best friend officially over her self-imposed dry spell?"

"Yes—I mean no. Noah and I are officially together now, but we've chosen to take things slow."

"What? I think a spell of another kind has been cast on you. Are you feeling well? If you take things any slower, we'll be rewinding time."

"We agreed we think it should be special. We've decided on early December. That way we can get Thanksgiving out of the way—and I might have included Black Friday in that scenario." I wince. "But only because I love a deal."

"Amen, sister." She fans herself a moment with her fingers. "So December, huh?"

"Early December. Right before the holiday hustle and bustle. I'm thinking about taking a weekend off from the bakery."

"An entire two days off in a row?" she teases. "You do realize you're the only person in the bakery who's worked seven days a week since opening day."

"It's my baby. Nell put me in charge, and I don't want to let her down."

"You're letting me down—by scheduling sex. You've managed to take something exciting and spontaneous and turn it into something akin to a doctor's appointment."

"And I'm sure the doctor will be very, very thorough with his examination." I blink a wry smile. "Keelie, this is what works for us, and it's going to be great. Noah is great."

"Just remember, if you overthink something, you might actually ruin it. Trust me, spontaneous is the only way to go. But since you're insistent, I'll buy you a calendar for Christmas, and you can pencil him in to your heart's content."

"Make it a calendar filled with kittens and I'll be more than content."

"Sex kittens." She waggles her brows. "So, what's next with the investigation? Any more strip clubs, mobsters, or Jungle Rooms to explore? I think your homicide hustle is far more interesting than what you don't have going on in the bedroom with Noah. And just for the record, that boy really is a fox."

"Don't I know it." I strum my fingernails over the table a moment. "Next up in my homicide hustle is speaking with a woman by the name of Jules King. She worked with Collette down at the PR firm."

"Ooh, are we bringing more cookies to those suited-up cuties down in Ashford?" Her shoulders shimmy in giddy anticipation.

"No. I'm afraid I'll arouse too much suspicion if I go

back. Besides, I'm pretty sure they're sick of seeing me. I thought we should just try to run into her—you know, something natural."

"Something natural. And how do you suppose we do that?"

"We follow her. We leave the bakery at four, so we arrive in Ashford by five and hopefully we see her head to her car. Maybe she'll go to the supermarket, or a restaurant before she goes home?"

"Or maybe she'll head to the Jungle Room and I can see this delicious place for myself!"

Keelie has been more than upset that I opted to take Everett over her.

"Or maybe she'll head home and we can see a movie instead?" I offer.

"We can hit dinner at the Ashford Grill. You can have your favorite Gouda grilled cheese, and I'll get the mac and cheddar."

"Now that you mentioned grilled cheese, I'm sort of hoping she goes home."

"Me too."

JULES DOESN'T GO HOME. Instead, she heads straight to the Ashford Hard Body Gym where both Keelie and I pick up a day pass to "check out the facility." I no sooner thanked the woman who issued the pass than I asked where my friend Jules might have gone.

"The dark-haired woman? She's a part of the Monday night Skin Swim—water aerobics. The locker room is right through those doors. You'll have to lock up all your things. They have a strict no cell phone policy. The only things you can bring into the pool room are your towel and a smile."

And she wasn't kidding. Not a stitch of clothing is permitted during what the teenager monitoring the locker room door referred to as the *skinny dip hour.*

Keelie and I head down through the gym to the private entrance to the pool room with our towels wrapped around our bodies as if we just got out of the shower. And my goodness, I'm going to need thirty showers just to wash this day off me.

"We're going to swim naked!" Keelie trills. Her excitement for this event seems unrivaled by just about anything we've done before just as mine is waning.

"Yes, Keelie, we are. And please, for the love of all things holy, do not look at my bits and pieces." The walkway opens up to a cavernous room locked in a blanket of humidity. The stench of chlorine burns my nostrils—and I'm assuming it will be burning far more delicate places sooner than later. A mass of flesh congregates near the opposite edge of the pool, and a smattering of people are already enjoying the cerulean blue water, swimming fearlessly, expanding and retracing their limbs like a frog, the way my mother does at the lake in the summer.

Keelie leans in. "My goodness, this gives an all new meaning to the words *breast stroke*."

"I'm just thankful there are only a handful of men, and they all look about *ninety*."

Her lips crimp. "Too bad that hottie judge isn't here. I'd sure like to climb on his shoulders and play a game of chicken."

My stomach tightens when she says it. I'm not sure how I feel about Keelie crushing on my Everett.

GAH! *My* Everett? He's not my anything. He's ornery, curt, and hardly ever smiles. He's a brick wall of a man who is so far removed from his emotions it's— That image of him shedding tears after speaking with his father comes back to me. Everett has a heart. He just chooses to save it for those few and far occasions such as contacting the dead.

"Well, he's not here. Grandpa Moses is. So put away your happy hormones and help me get through nude swim. I'm pretty sure this is what PE in hell looks like."

A dark-haired girl cannonballs into the water before rocketing back to the surface with her tresses perfectly glossed back.

"This is heaven!" she shrills as she swims over to a

group of women all seemingly happy they were splashed in the face by her shock and awe campaign.

"That's *her*," I whisper to Keelie as we head for the small crowd at the end of the pool.

An older woman wearing nothing but a whistle around her neck eyes the two of us, riding her gaze up and down our towels with what feels like bitter judgment.

"We got newbies!" she hollers, and the sound of her voice reverberates throughout the room.

At once each pair of eyes looks our way, and I can feel my skin growing hotter than a dumpster fire.

Dear Lord, what did she have to do that for? It was bad enough I'd have to drop my towel at all let alone with an audience at rapt attention.

"What are your names, girls?" She gives her graying curls a quick scratch—the ones on her head. Sadly, this type of occasion does call for clarification.

Keelie waves as if old friends were greeting us. "Kiki and Lottie!"

The crowd offers us both a warm welcome as our monikers circle the room in an echo.

"*Kiki?*" I hiss at my best friend's new nickname, which I know nothing about.

"I wasn't about to tell them my real name. What if one of them steps into the Honey Pot Diner and says *hey, it's Keelie from the nudie pool!* This way I can say it was my twin sister *Kiki.*"

"You do have a twin, and her name is Naomi."

"Drats. I always forget about that."

The crowd bursts into spontaneous song set to the turn of "Happy Birthday," stopping both *Kiki* and me in our naked tracks.

"We welcome you, we do! We welcome you, we do! We welcome you, Kiki and Lot—tie! We welcome you, we do."

The last stragglers hanging around next to the pool quickly get into the water, and the entire lot of them turns their backs to us.

"First, they sing—and then they shun us," I whisper. "Such is life."

"My name is Carol!" The older woman swims against the crowd to join us. "Whenever we have new people, we offer up a warm welcome. We all know how hard that first time can be getting into the water, and seeing the class is only an hour long, we found that turning our backs makes the process go by a whole lot faster. So, go on and drop your towels and come on in. The water is fine!"

She promptly turns the other way, and both Keelie and I glower at one another as if the reality of what was about to transpire were suddenly upon us.

We count to three, and no sooner do our towels hit

the floor than we're both in the water. Thankfully, it's as warm as a bath.

The class gets underway, and I mosey us over to Jules who's stretching and panting with the rest of them.

"Hope you don't mind," I whisper as I take the spot next to her.

"Nope! It's all yours. The first time's the toughest, but after a month you'll have to remind yourself to get dressed in the morning." She chortles as if the struggle was real.

"Well, I doubt that, but thank you for your reassurance." I'm pretty sure if I start showing up to the bakery in the nude I'll find myself wearing a nice tight straitjacket. And here I've feared that psychiatric accouterment for entirely different reasons all these years.

The instructor, who turns out to be Carol, has us doing jumping jacks, and not only is water sloshing around freely but spare parts are jumping and bouncing, and it's an overall unnerving scene. My jumping jacks involve my arms snuggly fitted over my girls, but Keelie seems to find the exercise both freeing and hilarious.

I look over to Jules with a manufactured smile, and she winces at me as if I were smiling for all the wrong reasons.

This could not get more humiliating if it tried. The lengths I go to for my friends. Everett owes me years' worth of dinner for this. Although, even if he tried to give it to me, I wouldn't collect. I really do care enough about him that I don't want to see him rotting away in a prison cell.

"Hey!" I say brightly to Jules as the instructor has us switching things up and jogging underwater. "You look familiar."

Jules glances my way. "Yeah, you sort of do, too. Do you work at Endeavor?"

"That's where I've seen you." I slap the water as if punctuating the epiphany and end up splashing myself in the eyes. Chlorinated water really does have a bite to it. "I mean, I don't work there, but I was delivering cookies."

"The cookies! Yes! Now I know where I've seen you. You catered the awards ceremony, and I think I had some of your cookies at the funeral, too." She grimaces as we begin to punch the air together.

"Yeah, that was really tough."

"I can't believe they still haven't caught that killer," she huffs. "Everyone knows the Ashford Sheriff's Department is run by total incompetents."

"*Hey.*" Keelie looks as if she's about to throw a punch at a far more solid surface.

"*Kiki,*" I hiss before turning back to Jules. "You're right. But from what I hear, everyone and their brother had a beef with Collette. I guess they have quite the suspect pool to weed through."

Jules belts out a laugh as we proceed to sock the ceiling. "You got me there. I don't know one person who didn't have a chip on their shoulder because of her."

"Me either," I say while racking my brain. "With the exception of that girl, Jenna, who gave the eulogy. They sounded as if they had the ideal friendship."

"Yeah, right," Jules balks as we start in on squats. Side note: underwater squats are a snap compared to the on-land variety. And again, chlorinated water really does have a bite to it. "Jenna couldn't stand Collette toward the end. But I suppose death cured her of that and she plugged ahead and gave a great speech anyway."

My body seizes just hearing it. "What kind of beef could Jenna have possibly had?" I'm more or less talking to myself, but hey, if Jules wants to throw me a bone, I'm all ears.

"Never mind. It's actually pretty tawdry, and I guess it's best to let old sleeping dogs lie." She rolls her eyes at her analogy.

Tawdry? Old sleeping dogs?

"Mr. Rutherford!" Again, totally speaking what I'm thinking. But hey, it worked for me the first time.

"So, you know?" She makes a face as she swings left and then right.

"Oh yeah, I mean, Collette and I were kind of close." Dear Lord, forgive me for speaking lies about the dead. "I know all about that affair she was having. I guess

Jenna was her side girl for a while." *Side girl.* Just saying the words makes me shudder. It's more than enough to have two people in a bedroom without inviting an entire party. I know for a fact I'm not sharing Noah with anyone.

"That's the thing"—Jules says, indulging in a deep lunge in my direction, her lips just above the waterline— "Jenna wanted Rutherford for herself. She was doing everything she could to get that man away from Collette. But Collette, she had something special that he was coming back for time and time again."

I suck in a sharp breath at the revelation. "Do you think she's the one that poisoned Collette?"

"I don't know. I mean, like I said, just about everyone had a beef with her."

"Oh right. My beef was that she snagged a man I was dating right from underneath me." I shoot a look over to Keelie in an effort to silence her. The last thing I want to do is drag Everett into this further.

"The judge?" Jules submerges herself underwater and comes back up. "You do realize why she was bringing him around, don't you?"

"Black hair, blue eyes, and a commanding presence that screams he's large and in charge? I think I can figure it out."

She belts out a laugh. "It was to make Rutherford jealous. She made no secret about that to anyone who would listen in the lunchroom. She wanted him to give poor Patty the boot so she could take the prized position and be the new Mrs. Brad Rutherford."

A horrible knot forms in my stomach. "So she and Jenna were essentially locked in a game of tug-of-war."

"That's right. Only Collette is dead, so I guess she loses."

And Jenna has a solid motive for murder.

Carol blows her whistle, and bodies begin to plod toward the stairs.

Jules turns to leave. "Hey, you never mentioned what your beef with Collette was." I try to keep my voice light as if it was some morbidly fantastic game we were playing.

She shrugs. "She beat me out for VIP, but I'm already over it. It's not like you get a raise with the honor. Besides, Collette is gone. I've got it in the bag next year."

"One more thing." I tiptoe over—the underwater version of running. "Um, that kid, Josh? The one that tried to revive her the night of the ceremony. What do you think his beef with her was?" I know what Jenna said, but now I'm questioning whether or not she was a reliable narrator.

"He's a sweetheart who got caught up in Collette's dark web. I guess he tried to get in on the kink that she partook in down at some gross club in Leeds, but she turned him away. Collette was all about the older alphas.

Young boys never interested her much." She plods her way to the steps. "See you next time."

No, you won't.

She turns back around, giving me the full frontal, and I cringe as I cover my own delicate parts with my hands.

"Oh hey! We're having a company picnic at the community center in Ashford tomorrow at two." She says *picnic* with air quotes. "The entire company is shutting down early. Mr. Rutherford usually throws a holiday party complete with a Thanksgiving Day meal, but out of respect for our recent loss he's retitled the event. I'm sure everyone would really appreciate it if you brought some treats. I can clear it with accounting, and, of course, we'd pay you for it."

"I wouldn't hear of it. Consider it a gift from me to the firm." And what a gift it will be to have one more chance to speak with Jenna. I'm sure her nose is a foot long by now.

Jules takes off, and I ruminate over our conversation.

Josh is a sweetheart, and Jenna sounds like a snake. I have some serious questions. Thankfully, I'll revert to a tried-and-true method of getting answers from just about anyone.

Cookie platter to the rescue.

CHAPTER 14

"You do realize you look guilty," I say, looking directly into Essex Everett Baxter's big blue eyes as he hardens his gaze over mine.

The bakery is bustling, and I've been up since three, baking up a storm to fill the order for that impromptu company picnic while my mind reeled at a mile a minute ruminating over all of the potential suspects—this dapper man in front of me being one of them.

"I realize that." Everett shifts uncomfortably in his seat. "But like I said, Collette could not take pills. I knew that from way back when we dated. Everyone knows that about her. She handed me two capsules, which she said would cure her of the headache she felt coming on, and asked me to sprinkle them into that concoction you had everyone drinking."

I inch back in my seat. "Concoction, Everett, really?"

Lily waves to me from the counter. "The platters are ready." For me she doesn't so much as crack a smile, but for Everett, she not only grins like a cat with a canary snug between its teeth, she leans over dramatically, ensuring us a full view of those globes she's doing a lousy job of hiding in her sweater.

"Thanks, Lily." I wave a hand over Everett's face and break the spell Lily Swanson has over him. "Where did she get the pills?"

His jaw redefines itself as if my questioning went too far. "She asked everyone in that room for pills, Lottie. I don't know. Maybe one of her friends plucked them out of her purse."

"Friends? Believe me, Collette had no friends." My eyes spring wide. "Jenna!"

"Yeah, maybe her. I don't know where they came from, but eventually the pills made their way to Collette."

"Okay, this is a good start. Now help me load up my trunk with cookies." I stand, and he follows.

"Where are you going?"

"We're headed to the Endeavor company picnic."

Everett's nostrils flare at the thought. "I have an idea. I'll drop the platters off, and you work on that recipe for the contest this Saturday."

"Aren't you a gentleman. It's almost as if you want me to stay out of the investigation. Say? You haven't been speaking to that ex-stepbrother of yours, have you?" Everett's entire world seems to be comprised of exes in every capacity.

He doesn't bother with a response. He doesn't bother with so much as lifting an eyebrow. Instead, he helps me load up my truck, and we hightail it down to the Ashford Community Center.

THE ASHFORD COMMUNITY CENTER is at least ten times the size of the community center in Honey Hollow. It has a fresh paint job, new glossy floors, and actual chandeliers in lieu of fluorescent lighting. Bodies fill the room to capacity, and the room is thick with the scent of turkey. Mr. Rutherford spared no expense. It's an entire Thanksgiving Day buffet with not only the famous bird on the menu but mashed potatoes, gravy, cranberry sauce, green beans, biscuits, marshmallow yams, and an entire litany of additional side dishes to ensure a terrific feast.

Everett helps me land the dessert platters to the side, and soon enough there are hordes of people henpecking at them. In addition to the cookies, I brought over several pumpkin and pecan pies. You can't really have a Thanksgiving celebration without them. Plus, this way, I'm hoping to win over a few new customers, too. Lord knows I'm already up to my eyeballs with pie orders for next week, but what's a few dozen more?

Jenna heads this way, her eyes fixated fully on that cookie platter, and I smack Everett on the arm.

"Here she comes. What should I say?"

"Ask if she's the killer, and if she says no, we can leave."

I glare up at him a moment.

"Lemon"—he gives a long blink—"you don't need any help from me. I see a slice of pumpkin pie with my name on it." He takes off, and I head over to Jenna who is building a precarious pyramid of nutty spice cookies and chocolate chip peanut butter swirls. She tops it off with a few Mexican wedding cakes and does a double take my way as I come into her line of vision.

Jenna is dressed in a low-cut dress with fall leaves printed over it, her lips are outlined bright red, and I can't help but wonder if she's looking to snag herself a Rutherford.

"Thank you so much!" Her eyes light up as she spots me. "You really do know how to bring the holiday cheer. Is there any way I can put in a special request for the next event?"

"Sure, I don't see why not." Although, I don't cater to prison, which is exactly where she'll be going once it's revealed that she's the killer. My goodness, I could be standing in front of a cold-blooded murderer! My body seizes with a momentary paralysis at the thought.

"Great. I really miss my mother's cranberry cheese ball cookies. She made them this time of year and I'm not sure which I miss more, the cranberry cheese balls or her!" She chortles as if it were hysterical.

"What kind of cheese?" I can't help it. Inquiring minds want to know.

"Two cups all American. Nothing fancy, just something tried-and-true. It goes great with turkey leftovers, too. I make me a mean turkey melt for about a week straight after the big day."

"That does sound delicious." The cookie not so much. "Hey, I have a question for you?" My word, I don't have a question for her! Who knows what hairy scary thing will evict itself from my throat next? Thinking on my feet never was my forte.

A thought comes to me.

"I heard a rumor that Collette was poisoned by some pills she was taking to alleviate a headache. The deputies said she got the pills from someone at the party. Did you see anyone give her the pills that night?"

GAH! If Jenna is the murderer, I just tipped her off to the fact that the sheriff's department is onto her. Dumb, dumb, dumb. This investigation stuff really is a learn-as-you-go kind of thing.

She gives a knowing nod. "Yeah, I heard the same thing. She asked everyone for medication. Poor thing forgot to put a couple of her migraine pills into her purse that night. She asked me, but I had one of those useless clutches with just enough room for my lipstick and car keys. I don't know who she got the pills from, but it could have been anyone."

She answered so smoothly and nonchalantly that either A: She's a psychopath killer. Or B: She's innocent. That really narrows down the field.

I lean in, my gaze intently fixed on hers. "I heard that kid, Josh—the one that gave her mouth-to-mouth—was just obsessed with her. Do you think he's a suspect?"

Her entire body trembles with a laugh. "If he killed her, I'm the new Mrs. Rutherford."

I laugh along with her. "Hey, speaking of which—they're not divorcing, are they?"

"Nope." Jenna takes an angry bite out of a chocolate chip peanut butter swirl. "That man is not going anywhere. Besides, Patty would rather hold onto him forever than let him off the matrimonial chain. This way she still has one hundred percent control of the estate."

"Where does that leave you? I mean, you love him, right? How could you not after spending so much time with him—you know." My voice grows quiet. That was the only delicate way to put it.

"Of course, I do." She shifts as she looks over at him as he laughs it up with a small crowd. "Who couldn't? He's a brilliant man and a generous lover."

Things I did not need to know.

"But he never chose me." Her eyes gloss over, and she puts down the cookies. "Excuse me." She takes off for the restroom as Everett comes back.

"You made her cry. Good work, Lemon. It looks as if your wicked work is done. Let's get out of here."

Josh heads over and helps himself to a slice of pecan pie.

"Not so fast." I speed over to him and am surprised at how tall he is up close. "Hello, I'm Lottie Lemon. I made the desserts. I was good friends with Collette."

His eyes widen a moment at the mention of her name. "That's nice. The cookies are good. I've had a few. I'm sure the pie is great, too. I'm a big fan of pie."

"Oh, it is." I give an awkward shrug after patting my own back. "Say, did you hear the rumor? They think

Collette was poisoned with pills that night—pills she was taking to cure her headache."

His jaw unhinges. "Pills?" He shakes his head at something or someone just past me, and I turn around to find Jenna flirting hard with Mr. Rutherford. "That's strange. I knew he was trying to dump her, but I didn't think he'd kill her."

"What do you mean?"

"I don't know." He lands a forkful of pie into his mouth and moans. "This is good. You really know your stuff."

"Thanks. But you have a theory? On the pills?"

"No theory. I saw Rutherford hand her the pills. But I didn't see her take them. I mean, she was complaining of a headache to anyone who would listen, so I didn't think twice about it." He shakes his head. "I'd bet good money it wasn't those pills that did it. The guy has a screw loose from hopping around behind his wife's back, but otherwise he wouldn't hurt a fly."

"That's quite a testimonial for a guy that had your girl." I'm not sure if I should have gone there, but the moment presented itself, and a visceral reaction is my best bet to get into the mind of a killer.

Josh sags as the fork slips from his grasp and onto his plate with a thud. "Collette wasn't my anything. I just thought she might give me some experience, you know? Get me started in the right direction. But she shut me down pretty hard. It's a good thing, though. If she hadn't closed the door in my face, I wouldn't have met Elizabeth. Today is our three month anniversary." He grins at someone just over my shoulder, and a short strawberry blonde with adorable freckles cozies up to him as the two of them take off into the crowd.

Josh seems fine. And in no way does he feel like a killer. In fact, he seems to be the one to have landed on top at the end of the murderous day. If he's been with his girlfriend for three months, then he probably didn't have a very high motive to kill Collette that night.

But who did?

I glance back to find an all too familiar face staring at me.

"Noah!" I jump with surprise. "Fancy meeting you here. I was just"—my finger points every which way—"cookies." I shrug.

"I see." His lids hang low, the way they do when he's filled with lust for me. Although, at the moment, he seems to be seething. "You were delivering cookies and questioning suspects." His dimples dig in, and suddenly I'd like to crawl right into one for shelter. "Lottie, you're tainting the investigation."

"But I found out that Jenna really didn't get along so great with Collette. She wanted—"

"Mr. Rutherford to herself. We already know that."

I frown at the thought of the infamous *we*. I hate the

thought of Ivy and Noah being anything let alone partners at the station. Noah and I are partners in crime. It's cute and it's catchy, and I refuse to give her the title.

"Did you know that Mr. Rutherford gave her the pills?"

Noah's eyes widen a moment before narrowing to slits. "I'm going to ask you once very kindly to stay away from Mr. Rutherford, and that includes anyone who works at Endeavor PR. Step back and let the professionals handle this."

A dark-haired woman tips her head my way, and I freeze.

"Hey, it's you again!" Jules King offers a cheery wave my way. "It was great seeing you at nude swim. Can't wait to work out with you again!" She dissolves into the crowd, and every last inch of me wishes I could dissolve right along with her.

"*Nude swim?*" Noah looks both perplexed and vexed by the idea. "Lottie, did you take off your clothes and swim with a bunch of strangers just to get ahead in this investigation?"

My mouth opens, but not a single intelligible word comes out.

"Steer clear, Lottie. I mean it." It comes out stern, just this side of anger. Noah is fuming, and suddenly so am I.

I dig a finger into his chest. "You're always telling me what to do." My voice raises a notch.

"And you're never doing it." His voice raises right along with mine.

"Don't expect that to change anytime soon."

I take off and find Everett before hauling him out the door.

Noah doesn't bother texting me an apology once I leave.

I guess if he's not bossing me around, he's got nothing to say.

I'm fine with that.

Mostly.

all in Honey Hollow is in full icy swing. By the time we get back into town, the bakery is closing for the day, so Everett and I picked up a pizza at Mangia on the way home. I can't help but feel as if I'm cheating on Noah by doing so. Pizza was our thing. Sure, we only partook together on the one occasion, but it was supposed to be a repeat effort on our part—which was going to lead to far more steamier repeat efforts in December.

Everett pulls into his driveway at the same time I do, and coincidentally the same time Noah does across the street. For a moment I think I should just run into my rental, grab Pancake, and hide under the covers, but the far more pragmatic part of me, the part that is half-ravenous for an extra sauce, extra cheese, veggie pizza walks the rest of me next door to Everett's in plain sight.

Everett grunts as he stares off in Noah's direction. "Why is my stepbrother glowering at me?"

My lips part, but I can't bring myself to tell him that Noah is most likely fuming about the pizza being our thing.

"Because he's hungry and you're not in the mood to share with him," I say as we head into his toasty home. Everett has the entire place decorated with gray and black furniture, a coffee table made of stainless steel, and that's exactly where we set the pizza box down.

"If you and Noah are having problems, I don't want to know about them."

"Good. Because I'm in no mood to share, myself."

"So, did you crack the case? I'd like to head back to work on Monday. I'm not cut out for nature walks and stepping into a bakery in the middle of the afternoon. No offense."

"None taken. And I don't know about cracking the case. It seems the harder I try to crack it, the tougher it gets. Collette led a complicated life that led a lot of people to the brink of madness. I mean, for all practical purposes you could be the killer."

He growls as he takes an angry bite of his pizza. Those hooded lids look ready to kill—*me* for delivering the news.

"But realistically, it could be just about anyone else as well. It turns out, Jenna Hatfield wasn't exactly on the best terms with Collette. She wanted Mr. Rutherford to herself. Collette, however, wasn't about to give up her big boss boy toy, and that's why she was showboating you whenever she got the chance—in an effort to make him jealous. Hey"—I snap my finger over at him—"I bet that's why they were arguing that night."

"Could be."

"Anyway, it was Rutherford who gave her the pills."

Everett nearly chokes on his next bite.

I lift a finger. "But Josh Normandy didn't think Mr. Rutherford would hurt a fly."

Everett chews on the thought, literally. "So what you're saying is that there could have been two sets of pills or—"

"Or someone switched them."

"Did you confide any of this to Noah?" he says it low and measured as if he knew the truth before he asked the question—and knowing Everett, he did.

"Why would I? He and Ivy are running a professional investigation. They certainly don't need me. What would I know? I'm just a baker."

His lips twitch as if he were about to shed a grin. "Don't underestimate yourself." He lifts his pizza my way as if he were toasting me. "I certainly won't make that mistake twice."

"Noah doesn't seem to mind doing it. In fact, he's making quite the habit of it."

"He's not underestimating you, Lemon. It's quite the opposite. He knows what you're capable of. He also knows what the bad guys are capable of."

"Bad guys?"

"Yes, Lemon, they're bad. And you are good. Too good to get in the way of some psychopath killer." There's a sternness in his tone, that serious look on his face. "How about we walk across the street and share some pizza and theories with Detective Fox?"

"No," I say it so fast and hard the sound reverberates off the walls.

"You're stubborn."

"Only as much as you are ornery."

He presses a genuine smile, and it's so rare I pause to memorize it.

It extinguishes itself in a moment. "There's a killer out there, Lemon."

"And I'm going to catch 'em."

Everett growls as if the thought angered him on some level. "Or they'll catch you."

"Touché."

But they're not going to catch me. Because I'm pretty certain they feel as if they've gotten away with murder.

And if any more time passes—they just might.

JUST BEFORE I dress for bed, and right after I give Pancake a second helping of his Fancy Beast cat food, there's a light knock at the door.

A prickle of excitement rides through me as I scoop Pancake up and interrupt his dinner number two. This sweet cat is so cute he could get me to rob a bank if he wanted.

"Well, who could that be?" I trill as we head to the door. I peer through the murky glass between us, and the porch light seems to be shining down on a familiar dark head of hair. "I bet it's Noah"—I whisper—"with his tail tucked between his legs and a big fat apology just waiting to stream from his mouth."

I swing the door open wide and jump back a little once I see it's not Noah. It's not Everett either. It's tall, lanky Josh Normandy with a phone in his hand.

"Hope you don't mind me showing up, but I've got something to show you."

I shoot a quick glance across the street and spot a figure in the window at Noah's house and feel a sense of relief.

"Sure, what is it? Does it have to do with the case?"

The case. I hate how clinical it sounds. Collette was a person, like her or not, and she's dead. Murdered in cold blood right there in the open for everyone to see.

"My aunt lives a couple of houses from Collette's place. It's how I met Collette in the first place. And once she told me how exciting it was to work for Endeavor, I took an internship right out of college, and that's how I ended up at the company." He glides his thumb over his phone and pulls up a picture before turning the screen so I can see it. "My aunt's security camera caught this. It's a still shot from the night she was murdered. There's footage of you there too with your boyfriend or your brother getting some stuff together. My aunt says he was doing some work at the house and probably wanted to get his tools before they put the place on lockdown."

My heart lurches in my throat. "Your aunt would be right. How did you know where I lived?"

He shakes his head as if it were a given. "My aunt knows everything. Anyway, this car showed up last that night. First, there was you and your boyfriend, then there was Jenna Hatfield who came out with a bag. My aunt thinks she was cleaning out the unmentionables— something about women having an agreement to do just that in the event of an untimely demise."

I twist my lips. "Your aunt really is perceptive."

He gives a light laugh. "Yes, well, she's got a theory on why this last car showed up, too." He hands me the phone, and I examine it under the porch light. A light gray luxury car I can't quite place and a dark shadow emerging or getting into it. "That's Rutherford. That's his Buick. And see this thing in his hand?" He points to a rectangular object. "That's a briefcase. A briefcase he didn't have when he went in."

A breath catches in my throat. "So that's where it went. What's your aunt's theory, if you don't mind me asking?"

"She says a man like Rutherford needs to keep his name out of the news because it could spook his investors."

"She's right again. Does she think he killed her?" I've asked everyone else. I don't see why Josh's all-knowing aunt should be left out of the morbid fun.

He glances over his shoulder in the direction of Collette's home in the not too far distance. "She doesn't think so. But she doesn't think whoever did it meant to kill her at the ceremony."

"But that's where you said he gave her the pills."

He shrugs. "And like I also said, I doubt Rutherford did this. Anyway, I want to keep my own nose out of it so I'm not turning this in to the police. I don't think it's big evidence. The deed was already done. Goodnight." He jogs back to his hatchback and speeds off down the street.

Pancake lets out a mean *rawrr*, and I glance right at Noah before stepping in and shutting the door.

"Well, now everything is just as clear as mud," I say, rocking my favorite ball of fur and nuzzling his face to mine. "Rutherford wanted any proof of his dalliances out of her house before the police got there—so much so that he risked getting caught doing it. I guess he values his position as CEO. Ticking off the board of directors could land him in the unemployment line. And he's no spring chicken."

I plop on the couch with Pancake and turn on the television, hoping that something will start to make sense soon.

But it doesn't.

Collette Jenner isn't allowed to be Honey Hollow's first cold case—not when Everett's career is on the line. And as much as Noah wants me to step back, there's no way I can stop now—at least not without speaking to Rutherford one more time.

And then I'll fill Noah in on everything I know and step back and let the professionals handle this.

Although, Detective Fairbanks and Detective Fox haven't solved a single case together yet.

Maybe I'm the professional after all.

CHAPTER 16

With a chill in the air, a thicket of dark clouds circling Honey Hollow, fall tourist season in full swing, and Thanksgiving just around the corner, the Cutie Pie Bakery and Cakery is at maximum customer capacity on Friday.

Lily comes back to the kitchen where I'm frantically reworking my famous pumpkin pie recipe, trying my best to put some fancy spin on it for tomorrow's contest.

"You've just had another thirty orders for pies today. If this keeps up, you'll have to bake five hundred pies by Thanksgiving—and that's pumpkin *and* pecan."

"We're not open on Thanksgiving. All pie orders are to be picked up by closing next Wednesday night—and don't tell anyone, but I'll be here an hour after closing in the event anyone gets stuck in traffic. As for orders"—I think on it for a minute—"keep taking them until next Monday night. I put in an extra-large order last week, and I'm pretty sure I can make whatever needs to be done twice over. I've never ordered holiday stock on my own, but Keelie helped me wrangle it together. We're going to be fine." I look to the staff and feel a pang of grief for them. "I'm fine with pulling crazy hours, but I feel terrible asking anyone else to do it with me."

"I'll do it." Lily shrugs. "It's easy. I've seen you do it. You do the hard part and mix the ingredients, make the crust, and I'll fill the pies and put them in the oven. It's not rocket science, Lottie."

"You'd do that for me?" I must be bordering on delirium if this makes me happy.

"Yes, I would do that for you. I happen to like my job. It's easy, it smells like cinnamon all the time, and I eat a free cookie on all my breaks. What more could a girl ask for?"

"Well, I'm glad you're content." I scour the island and

wrinkle my nose at the mess I've made. "I wish I was. I really want to impress those judges tomorrow."

"Please, you're coming home with the van. We both know it." She cranes her neck at the customers. "Isn't your sister dating Tanner Redwood?"

I growl just at the mention of his name. "Using the term loosely, yes."

"He's been here for an hour pawing all over some girl just out of high school. He's such a creeper. I have no idea what Lainey sees in him."

"Ditto to that." I hustle my way over to the front and, sure enough, seated under my romantic twinkle lights are Tanner the hair flipper and some pretty young thing who hasn't crested puberty. I'm about to toss the spatula in my hand as if it were a throwing star when the bell on the door chimes and in walks my mother and sister— and I couldn't be happier to see them.

Tanner jumps to his feet and wraps his arms around Lainey in a twirling embrace while his underage para- mour makes a break for it, dashing into the windy evening with nothing more than half a sweater and a miniskirt. Doesn't he realize where he is? Clearly, if he doesn't fear me, I haven't done my job right.

Tanner presses a heated kiss over Lainey's lips, and she pulls away with a half-hearted giggle.

"Lottie"—he points hard my way—"you got good eats. I'll put in a good word for you with the Parks and

Recs holiday committee." He nods my mother's way. "Miranda. Lovely seeing you again." He blows a kiss my sister's way and jets out the door.

"Good riddance," I say under my breath.

Lainey is quick to wave me off. "Tanner is a sweetheart."

I'm about to say something about the girl he was with but think better of it. Tanner is the two-timer. Who cares whether that girl has knowledge of my sister or not. He does. And he still chooses to behave that way.

"Tanner is something, all right." I lift a brow her way.

"How are the pies coming?" she asks as both she and my mother head behind the counter and follow me to the kitchen.

"I'm baffled. I'm thoroughly confused as to what I should do. A part of me says I should pull out all the stops. But another far more rational part of me knows you shouldn't mess around with a pumpkin pie until it's unrecognizable."

Mom takes off her coat and replaces it with an apron. "Oh, honey, you and I both know your standard pumpkin pie recipe is miles better than anyone else's. In fact, it makes a store-bought pie taste as if someone pureed last night's dinner."

"Mother." Lainey groans. "That's disgusting." She looks to me. "But she's right. And we're still on for Thanksgiving, right?"

"Yes, I'm determined to have it at my new home. I've already invited the two of you, and you're both welcome to invite dates."

Lainey plucks an oatmeal raisin cookie off the cooling rack. "Who *you* bringin'?" She gives a playful wink as she takes a bite.

Mom waves my sister off. "She's bringing Noah. Lottie has an official plus one these days—a bona fide detective no less. And you better believe I'm telling everyone about it." She giggles my way. "I'm just tickled to see you so happy. So, who did you decide gets the judge?" Mom shakes her shoulders as if she were throwing her hat into the ring.

"I don't get to decide that. In fact, I may not have an official plus one at Thanksgiving because I might not have an official plus one anymore." My voice cracks, and both Mom and Lainey ensconce me on either side.

Lainey pulls me over by the chin. "What happened? That boy is mad about you, and if you try to tell me something else, I may not believe you."

Mom gives my hand a quick tug. "I'm sure it's nothing. I can't tell you how many misunderstandings your father and I had. But, rest assured, the best is yet to come." A naughty grin percolates on her lips. My mother and father rarely if ever raised their voices. The image I have in my mind regarding them was a happy, playful couple. How I wish my father were still here to have fun with her, with us all.

"Trust me, it's no misunderstanding. He thinks I'm getting in too deep with this investigation, and I think I've come across a few valuable tips that might actually help catch whoever is responsible for this."

Mom hums like a defunct motor, her entire body gyrating as she struggles to keep a lid on her thoughts. "I'm just going to come out and say it. You need to leave well enough alone. It's a darn near miracle that the people of Honey Hollow didn't shun you after something you made landed a woman dead right in front of a live audience."

Lainey gasps. "Mother! The woman was poisoned! And the sheriff's department cleared both the bakery and Lottie of any wrongdoing."

"That's not the point." Mom picks up a spatula and begins stirring a bowl full of pumpkin pie filling, igniting the air with the scent of cinnamon and spices. "The point is, she nearly lost her business because of this maniac, and if he or she finds out Lottie is meddling, she might lose something far more valuable." She shakes her curls my way. "We can replace the bakery. We can't replace you."

"You sound an awful lot like Noah."

Lainey tips her head to the side and coos as if a

kitten just crawled out of a bowl behind me. "He really does care about you, Lot. You are one lucky girl."

"I know I am," I whisper as I look at pie shells waiting to be filled.

Mom and Lainey help me bake a few pies, and while doing so we discuss who's bringing what to my Thanksgiving party next week. Lainey suggested we eat at three sharp so we can spend the rest of the evening online shopping, and I wholeheartedly agree.

Mom gives me a hug as we lock up the bakery. "Don't worry about a thing tomorrow. Both your sister and I will be there to cheer you on. Rest assured, you're going to win."

"I hope so," I say, lacking the proper enthusiasm. It's not the win I want. It's the killer—and Noah's killer lips back on mine. Not necessarily in that order.

"You will. There is just so much to look forward to!" She gifts me a kiss before trotting off to her car. I stand there under the stars, the glacial wind nipping at my neck.

There certainly is a lot to look forward to.

But not for Collette.

In fact, she may not even get to look forward to justice.

CHAPTER 17

⁂

*T*he Thanksgiving Pumpkin Pie Bake-off is held in the state-of-the-art kitchen in the heart of Ashford Culinary School. There are thirty participants this year and a panel of nine judges, all of whom I'm sure will be hard to impress.

"Thirty participants," I lament to Keelie as we unload all of the ingredients onto my newly assigned workstation. The inside of the culinary school kitchen looks every bit like a studio, and good thing, considering the fact this event is televised on a local cable channel.

I spot Crystal Mandrake looking every bit the superstar with her chef's hat and army of sous chefs. Her blonde hair is pulled back into a hairnet, and her cinnamon-colored skin glows against the hot pink lipstick she's got on. Her apron is encrusted with rhinestones with the word *winner* emblazoned across the front.

Keelie leans in. "At least she's subtle. Don't worry. You've got this, Lottie."

My mother kept announcing spontaneously, *my daughter, the star*, over and over again on the ride to Ashford. She and Lainey commuted with Keelie and me, and now, looking at how serious my competition looks, I'm regretting not driving all by my lonesome in the event I want to cry all the way home. I usually do my best not to cry in front of people if I know it's going to make them uncomfortable, and since I've never run into a situation where it wouldn't, I usually do all of my boo-hooing in a closet somewhere, or in bed with Pancake. Although, I haven't boo-hooed once since that furry handsome little man came into my life. I wish I could have had Pancake at every age and stage of my existence.

"Relax," Keelie whispers. "You're going to do just fine."

"At least I have a great cheering section." I glance up

where Lainey and my mother are currently holding up a sign that reads *Team Lemon*.

"You sure do. And it's going to be expanding in about an hour or so. I've taken the liberty of inviting a couple of strong, handsome men to watch you drive home in that new ride of yours."

"You did?" I moan at the thought of seeing Noah and Everett here. "It's going to make me nervous. And believe me, I'm plenty of that all on my own."

"Nervous? About what? Lottie, this is your element. Pie is a part of your cellular makeup. And have you tasted that crust you make? People would gladly have that as their last meal."

"That's grisly."

"That's true."

We finish up all the prep, and soon enough I make the crust and the fillings. I bake the crust shell just enough to give it some firmness before pouring in my signature recipe. It looks so smooth and creamy and smells as if the entire fall season were melted into this one delicious pie filling, I'm half-tempted to sit down and eat it with a spoon.

Hey? Maybe I could bottle this and sell it as comfort food? Although, on second thought, you can catch all sorts of things from uncooked eggs, and Lord knows I don't need another poisoning on my hands.

Just as I'm finishing up and setting my two pies into

the oven, all contestants are called to the front to meet the judging panel. It's a blind reveal in the event we try to cater to the judges and their personal preferences. It's not uncommon for judges to switch out from year to year just to keep those who participate in these kinds of contests on their toes.

The emcee of the evening is a tall, stocky man who looks as if he's a pie lover indeed named Jeremy Nicolson, a star chef himself and who also happens to teach at the culinary school.

Jeremy introduces the judges down the line, along with their interests, and before he gets to the end, I do a double take at the woman with the tight bun, the excess skin on her face pulled back because of it, and those twisted tight bright orange lips. It's none other than Patricia Rutherford. I'm both relieved and enlivened by the sight of her. And here I thought today would be a waste of the investigation. But as soon as we're excused, I'm going to say a quick hello. Since the judges will sample the pies blindly, there are no restrictions on mingling with them.

"And on the end"—Jeremy Nicholson gurgles out a drum roll—"we have the ever so lovely Mrs. Patricia Rutherford whose interests include baking, knitting, reading eighteenth century poetry, and horticulture."

I glance my mother's way. Patricia would fit right in with her Horticulture Hotties. I'm about to laugh the idea off when suddenly my lungs seize, my muscles freeze solid, and I have very bad case of tunnel vision. All I see is Patricia Rutherford hunched over a patio table somewhere grinding up dehydrated wolf's bane into a fine powder.

"It can't be," I whisper as bodies begin to mill about freely once again.

Someone from the stands calls my name, but I don't turn around. I'm one hundred percent focused on the task at hand.

Patricia gives a trace smile as I step in front of her.

"I remember you." I try to sound friendly, sound excited over this, but there's not a cheery note in my tone. In fact, I sound frightened, highly disappointed that this poor woman would be driven so far.

"Excuse me?" She takes a careful step back, her lips trembling with the question.

"I remember you." I shake my head at her in disbelief as I follow her to a dark corridor.

"I remember you, too, Ms. Lemon. You certainly know your way around a kitchen." She looks past me. "Now, if you'll ex—"

"And you know your way around a garden, don't you?"

She stops dead in her tracks, and her eyes widen a notch as she takes me in and inspects me from head to toe as if surveying what I might know.

She tries to take a step to my right and I block her at the pass, but instead of bulleting past me, she turns around and bolts down the corridor. A door opens and closes in the distance, and I'm left with silence.

"Patricia, wait!" I call out as I take off after her. The hall is painted black, and the doors lining the hall are painted the same dismal color. I quickly open and close a few of them, but they lead to a broom closet and a pantry. There are at least a dozen doors between me and the end of the hall. I pat my pockets down for my phone to call Noah, but I don't have it on me. It's buried in my purse, in Lainey's possession for safekeeping.

The figure of a man appears at the end of the hall, and I breathe a sigh of relief at the sight of him.

"Everett!" I run over and throw my arms out for a quick embrace, falling right through him.

It's not Everett. That would explain the fact he's illuminated from the inside.

"Edward! Do you know where she went?"

He nods.

"Take me to her!" I hiss.

He turns to his left and touches his ghostly hand to the nearest door. I don't waste any time. I simply speed right in. I take a few stumbling steps inside, then proceed with caution as I take a look around. There's nothing but a dull blue glow of natural light streaming in from the tiny windows up near the ceiling. It's an oversized kitchen, a classroom I'm assuming, and in the middle of the gargantuan space stands an oversized island made of stainless steel.

"Patricia?" I call out but am met with silence. I glance back to Edward, but he's vanished. A lot of good that does me.

A tower of boxes lines my left. And in front of me, suspended on the wall, is a row of cutlery secured to a magnetic strip. I speed over to arm myself in the event I need it.

"Stop right there." Patricia emerges from behind the boxes, the steely blade of a chef's knife secured tightly in her hand.

"You did it," I say breathless as I look to this crazed version of the demure woman I've come to know her as. "You killed Collette." The words stream from me numb with shock. "You were the last person I suspected. But you did it because your husband was having an affair. You let the world think you didn't care and you did. You very much cared indeed."

A ripple of laughter emits from her, something dark and maniacal. "You stupid little thing. I didn't care about that silly girl, just like I don't care about you."

"Of course, you didn't care about Collette. That's why she's no longer with us," I hiss, my adrenaline spiking to unsafe levels.

"I didn't kill her, you ridiculous idiot! None of it was

intended for that girl. What a waste of all my precious time. Had I known he was asking for her, I wouldn't have given it to him."

My mouth falls open. "Oh my word." It feels as if the floor is slipping out from underneath me. "You were trying to kill your husband."

Those orange lips of hers flicker a short-lived smile. "Now you're catching on."

"But he wasn't the one with the headache. He passed the pills along to Collette. Only she didn't do well with pills, so she had Everett dump them into her drink. Wolf's bane."

She flinches when I say the name as if I struck her.

"You grew it. You dumped the original contents of those capsules and filled them with the wickedness you grew for this very purpose." I take a step in close, and she lifts the knife another notch. "Why not just divorce him? Isn't that what you wanted? To get away from him?"

"After thirty years of marriage? So some whore could get half of what we've taken a lifetime to build? I'm the only one who will reap any benefits when Bradford dies, and he will die." Her eyes widen hypnotically as they remain pinned on mine. "As will you." She snatches me by the wrist with her free hand and pulls me close with a violent yank. "Say your prayers. You will soon meet your maker."

I try to pull my arm out of her hold, but she's remarkably strong. I reach up, pulling her head down hard by the hair as Patricia cuts the air next to me with the knife. The blade hooks into my sweater at the waist, and she struggles to free it for a moment.

"Don't do this!" I shout, hoping someone other than Patricia will hear.

"You gave me no choice!" She slashes the knife over my stomach and I jump back, narrowly avoiding the blade. I lift my arm up hard and break her hold over me, my knee reflexively rising up with it in an effort to protect myself.

"You won't get away with this. You have to know that. Hurting me will only make things worse." I manage to grab ahold of her wrist just below the handle of the knife and we wrestle for it, our limbs locked above our heads in a struggle for power, for survival.

Patricia lunges at me with her body and knocks me off balance. Her arm falls hard over me as the knife slices through the sleeve of my sweater. Without hesitating, I knock her to the wall, pinning her to it with my body, and I pluck the knife right out of her hand.

The sound of footsteps thundering in this direction comes closer by the second.

"*Lottie!*" A familiar deep voice resonates from the other side of the wall.

"In here!" I cry as I glance to the door, and Noah bursts in with his hand across his waist.

In an instant the roles are reversed, and my back is pressed to the wall, the blade of the knife to my neck as Patricia Rutherford holds me down as efficiently as a wrestler. A move I'm sure my sister, Meg, would approve of.

"*Freeze!*" Noah holds the barrel of a gun our way, his legs parted, straddling the weapon he's holding erect before him.

The tip of the blade pinches my flesh. That horrifying barrel only seems to grow larger. Never in my life have I been so afraid. Never in my life have I been so utterly helpless. Can't breathe. Can't feel a thing. The ground feels as if it's rising to meet me.

My knees give out, and Patricia jerks the knife away. I roll my body into hers and she topples to the floor, hitting her head with a hard thud. Without putting too much thought into it, I flick the knife out of her hand and send it spinning across the room.

"*Lottie!*" I look up to find Everett bursting in behind Noah, along with a couple of deputies with their weapons drawn.

"It's safe," Noah barks, and every weapon in that room slowly disappears.

A flock of deputies are on Patricia at once. Noah pulls me to the side and wraps his arms around my body in a hard embrace, his lips running a line of kisses up and down my cheek. He pulls me back and inspects me, his eyes pausing on the gash in my sweater.

"You're hurt."

"No, it's nothing."

"Lemon." Everett steps in close, and Noah loosens his hold on me. "What the hell happened?"

"She confessed," I say it loud enough so the arresting deputies can hear. "She was trying to kill her husband, and he gave the pills to Collette. The poison was never meant for her. It was meant for Brad Rutherford. Everett, you're clear. You can get back on that bench come Monday," I pant through a smile. "I saw him again. He helped me." My chest heaves as I breathe the words below a whisper.

Noah gives my arms a gentle squeeze. "Who did you see? Was it Mr. Rutherford?"

My mouth opens as I look to Everett and shake my head. "I guess, it might have been. I don't really know who it was."

Everett pulls me into a partial embrace. "I'm glad you're safe, Lemon. I owe you." He takes off, and Noah reels me back in.

"Lottie." Noah inches his head back so he can get a better look at me. "I'm sorry we had a disagreement."

I shake my head and press a finger to his lips. "I'm sorry. I know that you want to keep me safe."

His eyes close for a moment, and it feels as if he takes the light from the room. "I was terrified when I found you with a knife to your neck. I'm glad you're safe, but if I didn't get here in time..." His Adam's apple rises and falls.

"I'm sorry I put you through that. But I'm safe and Collette's killer has been caught and is officially off the streets."

"You did it." A sly smile creeps up his cheek.

"But I'm sure you and Ivy were about to close in." I can't help but tease him.

A dull laugh rattles through his chest. "Actually, we just closed in on the perpetrator who vandalized Everett's place." He averts his eyes as if his find embarrassed him on some level.

"Don't keep me in suspense. Who was it?" My heart starts to drum once again, but it doesn't have anything to do with the perpetrator—it's one hundred percent this gorgeous man who's holding me in his arms.

"Steven Jenner."

"Her brother!"

"The funeral left him feeling helpless, and he confessed to his mother. She called this morning and apologized on his behalf. There will be a fine, and it's up to Everett if he wants to file charges."

"I doubt he will. He's pretty forgiving."

"Are you?" He winces.

"Always. The only thing I won't forgive is if you don't kiss me right this second."

A lascivious grin blooms on his lips. Noah takes my mouth as if he owned it, hot and reckless, and he does very much own it. He can have his way with my mouth, and in less than a month, he can have his way with the rest of me, too.

We make our way back to the competition just in time to see Crystal Mandrake holding the keys to her brand new cargo van, and I'm okay with it.

She can have the van.

Everett can take his rightful place on the bench, and I can have the first good night's sleep in a very long time.

CHAPTER 18

here are so many things that I am thankful for, my family, my friends, the special man who stole my heart. But this time of year has me thankful for even the smallest of pleasures, a smile from a stranger, seeing the joy a cookie can bring a child, a cozy fire, a slice of pie, a mug filled with pumpkin spice everything. I am so very thankful for the town I call home, for the people who reside in it, and the fact that now we can all sleep a little bit sounder at night.

If I've found anything to be true, it's that love conquers all. Noah and I leaped over this latest hurdle. We are still trying to find our parameters, file down the rough edges of who we are. But we're okay with that as long as we are on our way to becoming who we're destined to be—together.

After a breakneck pie-baking marathon, after all three hundred sixty-five pies were picked up—more or less on time—I closed down the shop last night and spent my first full day off from the bakery cooking up a storm in my new kitchen. Noah and Everett helped with the turkey, stuffing, and gravy. My mother brought the mashed potatoes and candied yams, and Lainey brought the green bean casserole—sans Tanner who didn't bother to show even after he said he would. It's probably for the best. The less Lainey sees of him the better. And, of course, I baked a couple of pies—two pumpkin, two pecan.

Noah moans through a bite. "Best pie I've had in my life."

Everett lifts his fork as he savors a bite. "I agree." He looks my way. "You should really consider opening a bakery."

The room breaks out into a warm laugh.

Keelie and Nell stopped by for dessert, and Nell laughs the longest at Everett's little quip.

Nell lifts her cup of cider, and the rest of us follow suit.

"To the formidable Lottie Lemon." Her face breaks out into a series of comma-like wrinkles as she smiles with all she's got. "You are a wonder, and you have been ever since the beginning. Truly the one who steals your heart will have a treasure to behold, as we all do." She gives Noah a hint of a wink.

"I second that." Mom lifts her mug even higher. "Lottie, dinner was fantastic, dessert is divine—and no more stumbling upon dead bodies, missy!"

The room erupts into another round of joyful laughter.

"I'll drink to that." Noah touches his glass to mine, and we give a cheer as we sip cider next to a cozy fire, the scent of turkey and pumpkin pie still clinging thick in the air.

Everett clears his throat. "I've got something I'd like to say."

The room gifts him our full attention, and even Pancake wags his tail from the sofa, that perennially bored expression of his pinned right on Everett.

"Lottie, we've been through a lot this last month alone. You believed in my innocence even when others brought it into question." He pauses to glower at Noah. "You not only helped me work through some personal matters"—his quiet gaze says thank you all on its own—

"but you helped clear my name by catching a killer. I am indebted to you more than you will ever know, and as a small token of my appreciation, I hope you accept the gift I have for you."

"A gift." I touch my hand to my chest. "Everett, no. You didn't have to do that. I'm fiercely loyal to my friends. Helping you was something that I felt I needed to do. Really, no gift is necessary."

"It's too late." He rises and steps away from the table. "If you'll excuse me, I'd like to go and get it." Everett takes off, letting in a brutally cold breeze in his wake.

Keelie presses out a nervous laugh. "Wow, Lot—you get the man, you bake a pie to die for, *and* you get prizes?" Her eyes tear up in an instant. "I couldn't think of a nicer person to receive all of the above and more. I love you."

"I love you, too. In fact, I love the entire lot of you and—"

The sound of a horn going off out front stops me cold. It toots three times fast once again, and our attention switches to the windows.

Lainey runs over and peels back the curtain. "Oh my word. Lottie Kenzie Lemon, get over here like yesterday."

The horn toots into the night, and I open the door to see something that I will never forget as long as I live. Parked in the street with the motor idling is a beautiful white cargo van. On the side of the pristine door are the words *Cutie Pie Bakery and Cakery. Fine confections, coffee, and more!*

"Essex Everett Baxter!" I shout his name like a reprimand as I race down the stairs.

Everett comes around and stands next to this mammoth display, and an entire jumble of words gets locked in my throat.

"It's my fault you didn't win that contest last week, Lemon. It's the least I could do to make it up to you."

"No!" My hands cover my mouth as a flood of emotions overtake me. I don't like to cry in front of anyone, but tears seem to be flowing without my permission. "You have to take this back. It's too much."

My mother comes alongside of me and presses a sweet kiss to my cheek. "Just say thank you, Lottie. It's a beautiful gesture."

My lips part as I glance to Noah, and he gives a hint of a nod.

"Thank you, Everett." I dive over him with a solid embrace. "As much as you don't want the world to know it, you are a very sweet man."

"Let's keep that as our little secret. Among other things," he whispers.

"You bet."

I take Nell and Keelie, my mother and Lainey for a ride around the block. And when we get back, Noah and

Everett haven't killed one another, so that's another thing to be thankful for.

One by one I say goodnight to them all with the exception of my two favorite gentlemen.

Everett looks to Noah and glances to the house. "You mind if I have a quick word with Lemon?"

"Not at all." Noah looks pained but willing to go along with it. "I'll go stoke the fire."

Everett waits until the front door shuts before taking a breath. "I wanted to thank you one more time for helping me out with my dad. You know, I never knew what a weight I was carrying around until I absolved it. He was a special man, and now I realize how lucky I was to have him in my life."

"That's beautiful." A light flickers behind him, and slowly a familiar form begins to take shape.

"Just wish I had one more chance to tell him myself. In fact, I'd like to tell him a lot of things. Catch him up on life."

I look past Everett at his glowing blue lookalike. It's as if a blue flame were lit up from within him.

"You can," I say. "He's right there." I point over at him, and the old man nods toward Everett's home and begins walking that way. "I think he's headed to your place. I'm not sure how long he's allowed to stay now that you're out of the woods, but I'm betting it will be long enough to hear whatever it is you have to say."

A quiet laugh bounces from him. "Wait up, Pops!" he calls out. "I guess I'd better go." He lands a chaste kiss to my cheek before heading down the street. "Thank you, Lemon. You really are the best."

I head back inside, and Noah and I warm one another by the fire while Pancake watches with a disapproving scowl from a pillow on the sofa.

I steal a bite out of Noah's lower lip and linger, running my fingers over the five o'clock shadow on his cheeks. "Guess what's coming right up?"

"Black Friday. I already know. I'm about to pounce hard on the electronics section of the internet. I've already gotten my eye on four different flat screens."

"Just four?" I laugh as I wrap my arms around the back of his neck. "I was thinking of something a little more exciting than a television. Like say, something very, very exciting about to take place at the beginning of December?"

"Ah, yes—the Parks and Recs Tri-City Community Christmas Party. Lainey mentioned that Tanner put in a good word for you and you got the gig."

I growl at the sound of his name. "I'd like to think I would have gotten it despite his efforts. But regardless, yes, that is just a hop and a skip away. But I was thinking of what might be happening later that night, after all of my cookies and pies have been delivered." My fingers walk up his neck, and I trace the outline of his lips.

Noah Corbin Fox has full, beautiful, soft lips—exciting, dangerous lips, and I can't wait to see what he can do with them once they're taken off their leash.

"You ready for this, Lottie?" His lids hood low, and there's a naughty connotation in his voice.

"Ready and willing," I say.

"It looks like we have a lot to look forward to."

"We do."

Noah crashes his lips to mine, and we sit by the fire, showing just how thankful we are to have one another in our lives.

Yes, it is a season of thanks—but with Noah by my side, it will be a lifetime of thanksgiving.

Now if only I can stop the ghosts, the dead bodies, from cropping up in my life, I really will have it all. The last thing I want is a few secrets of the dearly departed variety threatening to stop us before we ever really get the chance to begin. But this kiss right here suggests that Noah and I can never be torn apart.

The fire growls out with an earsplitting crackle as if it heard, and Noah and I pull apart for a moment. My stomach cinches with the seemingly insignificant action. It's unnerving, debilitating to think it might have been supernatural.

I bring his lips back over mine where they belong, and we let the fire in our hearts warm us for the brilliant future that lies ahead.

Another explosive crackle emits, this time ten times louder than the last, and we pull away again, nervous laughter filling our mouths.

A part of me believes that Noah and I will have a brilliant future.

But another part of me says we won't.

NEED MORE? Pick up Gingerbread & Deadly Dread (Murder in the Mix 4) and head back to Honey Hollow, NOW!

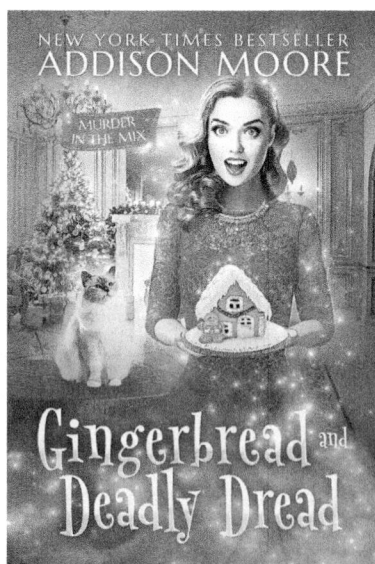

RECICE

Pumpkin Spice Latte
From the kitchen of the Cutie Pie Bakery and Cakery

*H*ey ho! Lottie Lemon here! There is nothing like fall in Vermont, the leaves, the crisp chill in the air—the even crisper apples—and the coffee to go along with it. Confession—as soon as August rolls around, I'm already craving pumpkin spice everything. So it shouldn't be a surprise to see more than a few pumpkin spice goodies making their appearance in my bakery. I like to keep the pumpkin lovin' rolling all the way until January. Here's my best recipe for my go-to drink in the fall. Feel free to enjoy this all year round. I do!

Ingredients

2 cups milk (your choice! Whole is best. Can be substituted with milk alternatives)
2 ½ tablespoons pumpkin puree
½ teaspoons pumpkin spice
2 tablespoons sugar (less or more to taste)
1 tablespoon vanilla extract
½ cup coffee (strong)
*Whipped cream to top it off with creamy style!

Directions

In a small saucepan combine milk, pumpkin puree and heat over medium flame until it's just about to boil. (Don't boil it!). Remove saucepan from hot burner and add pumpkin pie spice, vanilla, and coffee. Whisk until well combined. Pour into two coffee mugs and add whipped cream if desired (you can dust the whipped cream with pumpkin spice to jazz it up a little).

Happy fall!

BOOKS BY ADDISON MOORE

Murder in the Mix Mysteries

Cutie Pies and Deadly Lies

Bobbing for Bodies

Pumpkin Spice Sacrifice

Gingerbread & Deadly Dread

Seven-Layer Slayer

Red Velvet Vengeance

Bloodbaths and Banana Cake

New York Cheesecake Chaos

Lethal Lemon Bars

Macaron Massacre

Wedding Cake Carnage

Donut Disaster

Toxic Apple Turnovers

Killer Cupcakes

Pumpkin Pie Parting

Yule Log Eulogy

Pancake Panic

Sugar Cookie Slaughter

Devil's Food Cake Doom

Snickerdoodle Secrets

Strawberry Shortcake Sins

Cake Pop Casualties

Flag Cake Felonies

Peach Cobbler Confessions

Poison Apple Crisp

Spooky Spice Cake Curse

Pecan Pie Predicament

Eggnog Trifle Trouble

Waffles at the Wake

Raspberry Tart Terror

Baby Bundt Cake Confusion

Chocolate Chip Cookie Conundrum

Wicked Whoopie Pies

Key Lime Pie Perjury

Red, White, and Blueberry Muffin Murder

Honey Buns Homicide

Apple Fritter Fright

Vampire Brownie Bite Bereavement

Pumpkin Roll Reckoning

Cookie Exchange Execution

Heart-Shaped Confection Deception

Birthday Cake Bloodshed

Cream Puff Punishment

Last Rites Beignet Bites

For the full list please visit Addisonmoore.com

ACKNOWLEDGMENTS

HUGE and hearty thank you for diving into the MURDER IN THE MIX world once again! I hope Lottie and the fine folks of Honey Hollow met and exceeded your expectations and idea of a great time!

Running hugs to the fabulous Jodie Tarleton for your amazing eyes. You are so very generous and kind. I'm so wonderfully blessed to know you!

Gigantic thanks to the ah-mazing Kaila Eileen Turingan-Ramos. Please never leave me. I love you.

To the kind and wonderful Shay Rivera, beta of the year! I'm so grateful you still find time to read my work even though you have full and busy days of your own! Bless your beautiful eyes!

To my sweet sis, Lisa Markson the Great. You are simply the best.

To Paige Maroney Smith, I am forever in your debt. I'm wrapping myself around your ankles and never letting go. You're mine!

And last, but never least, thank you to Him who sits on the throne. Worthy is the Lamb! Glory and honor and power are yours. I owe you everything, Jesus.

ABOUT THE AUTHOR

Addison Moore is a *New York Times, USA Today,* and *Wall Street Journal* bestselling author who writes contemporary and paranormal romance. Her work has been featured in *Cosmopolitan* Magazine. Previously she worked as a therapist on a locked psychiatric unit for nearly a decade. She resides on the West Coast with her husband, four wonderful children, and two dogs where she eats too much chocolate and stays up way too late. When she's not writing, she's reading. Addison's Celestra Series has been optioned for film by 20th Century Fox.

f y ○

Printed in Great Britain
by Amazon